Runaway Road

USA *TODAY* BESTSELLING AUTHOR

DEVNEY PERRY

RUNAWAY ROAD

Copyright © 2019 by Devney Perry LLC

ISBN: 978-1-950692-09-5

This is a work of fiction. Names, characters, places and incidents are the product of the author's imagination or are used fictitiously. Any resemblance to actual events, locales or persons, living or dead, is coincidental.

Editing & Proofreading:

Elizabeth Nover, Razor Sharp Editing

www.razorsharpediting.com

Lauren Clarke, Creating Ink

www.creatingink.com

Julie Deaton, Deaton Author Services

www.facebook.com/jdproofs

Karen Lawson, The Proof is in the Reading

Judy Zweifel, Judy's Proofreading

www.judysproofreading.com

Cover:

Sarah Hansen © Okay Creations

www.okaycreations.com

ALSO BY DEVNEY PERRY

Jamison Valley Series

The Coppersmith Farmhouse

The Clover Chapel

The Lucky Heart

The Outpost

The Bitterroot Inn

The Candle Palace

Maysen Jar Series

The Birthday List

Letters to Molly

Lark Cove Series

Tattered

Timid

Tragic

Tinsel

Tin Gypsy Series

Gypsy King

Riven Knight

Stone Princess

Runaway Series

Runaway Road

Wild Highway

CHAPTER ONE

LONDYN

"Londyn, please. Please, don't do this."

Please, don't do this.

If I had a quarter for every time I'd heard that sentence from this man in the last eight years, I'd be a richer woman.

"Goodbye, Thomas." I ended the call. Since he usually called back five seconds after I hung up on him, I turned the damn thing off and tossed it across the bed to my best friend, who stood on the other side. "Here."

"Ack." Gemma fumbled it, she'd always been a butterfingers, and it fell unharmed onto the fluffy white down comforter. She snatched it up. "What do you mean, *here?*"

"Keep it. Smash it. I don't care. But I'm not taking it with me." I folded another T-shirt and laid it in my suitcase.

1

The entire thing was packed with brand-new clothes, most with the tags still attached. There wasn't a stitch of silk or satin to be found. Nothing I was taking required a press or steam and there sure as hell wasn't a pair of heels stuffed inside.

I had jeans. Normal jeans. I hadn't owned a pair in years. Now I had ten. Some had distressed patches by the knees. Some had frayed hems. Some were slouchy—or boyfriend, as the labels read.

Along with my denim, I had tees. White. Gray. Black. Navy. All the same colors as the suits I'd worn for years, but this time everything was machine-washable cotton. I might even wear them without a bra.

My wardrobe would no longer be a prison. Neither would this house. Neither would my phone.

"You have to take a phone, Londyn." Gemma planted her hands on her hips. Her cream suit was perfect—I used to have the same one. Her dark hair was styled in a tight chignon, exactly how I used to style my blond mane.

"No." I folded the last T-shirt. "No phone."

"What? That's—it's . . . insane. And stupid."

I shrugged. "We've both done it before."

"And we were both stupid before. We're lucky we didn't end up as skin suits." She threw her long arms out at her sides, huffing as she shook her head. "Take your phone."

"No."

"Londyn," she snapped. Gemma acted angry but her

2

anxious gaze spoke otherwise. She was simply worried. If I were in her Louboutins, I would be too. "How will I find you?"

"You won't find me. That's the point." I rounded the bed and took her pink-manicured hands in my own. I'd missed our standing date at the salon for the past three weeks and my nails were wrecked. I'd ripped off my shellac and chewed them to the nub. "I'm going to be okay."

She looked at me, standing three inches taller. "Please, don't do this."

"No," I whispered. "Not you too."

"Londyn," she whispered. "At least take the phone."

I squeezed her hands tight and shook my head. "I'm going. I need to go. You of all people should understand."

"Wait just a little longer. Let things settle down here," she pleaded. "People get divorced every day."

"They do." I nodded. "But this isn't about the divorce. It's me. I'm sick of this life."

"So you're running away?"

I rolled my eyes. "You make it seem so extreme for someone who's done the same, but yes. I am running away." *Again.* "Sometimes it's for the best."

She couldn't argue. She'd run away before and look at her now. Successful. Wealthy. Stunning. No one would suspect that she'd spent her teenage years living in a junk-yard outside Temecula, California.

"Ugh," she groaned. "Fine."

She didn't like this idea of mine, but she understood. My divorce had been brutal and heartbreaking. It had been the nuclear bomb to my life I'd needed. It was forcing a fresh start. Besides, I was good at starting over. I'd done it countless times in my twenty-nine years.

What was one more?

As of Thursday last week, I was single. I'd already changed my last name back to McCormack, and with my new driver's license in hand, I was not sticking around Boston any longer.

"I hate that you're doing this alone." Gemma sighed. "I'll worry."

"I'll be fine." I returned to my suitcase, folding a hoodie for the stack.

It was one of the few pieces I'd had in my closet that I'd set out to pack. It was thick and gray, the hems battered by a designer, not from use. The thing had no stretch. I'd worn it only once when Thomas had taken me sailing years ago, when we'd seemed happy.

This sweatshirt was a lot like my marriage. It looked cute but didn't quite fit.

I took the hoodie out of the suitcase and tossed it on the bed.

"What if you get hurt?" Gemma asked.

"Give me some credit." I rolled my eyes. "I have money. I have a car. I'm running away in style. It'll be a breeze."

"When are you coming back?"

Never. "I don't know."

"Will you call me? Check in periodically?"

"Yes, but you have to promise not to tell Thomas where I'm at."

She scoffed. "That son of a bitch comes anywhere near me, I'll rip his balls off."

I laughed. "There's my best friend. Glad to see some of the polish come off."

"Just with you." She smiled. "I'll miss you."

"I'll miss you too." I abandoned the suitcase and met her at the foot of the bed for a hug.

We'd been through a lot together over the last thirteen years. Gemma and I had met one night in an alley. She'd saved me from eating half a sandwich I'd dug out of a Dumpster.

There'd been times when she'd gone her way and I'd gone mine, but we'd ended up together in Boston. We'd become closer than ever, serving as each other's refuge as we'd climbed up the ranks of Boston's elite and wealthy.

I'd married into my money. Gemma had earned hers.

I finished packing, loading up my purse with the cash I'd taken out yesterday and my wallet. Then I zipped up my suitcase and hefted it down the hallway to the front door.

My keys were on the table in a dish. I took the bundle in my hand and removed only one to take along.

A car key.

"What if you don't find Karson?" Gemma asked, standing by my suitcase.

I stared at the silver key. "I'll find him."

I had to find him. I needed closure after too many years of wondering what kind of man he'd grown into from the boy I'd once known.

Past Gemma, the tile in the foyer gleamed under the crystal chandelier. The art on the wall was not my favorite, but Thomas had bought it at a charity auction, so at least it had been bought for a purpose beyond just decorating my lavish home—my former home.

I gave Gemma a sad smile. "This was the nicest place I've ever lived."

Thomas and I had a staff to take care of the mansion. A daily housekeeper cleaned and did laundry. A cook made whatever suited my fancy. A gardener kept the grass green and the flowers blooming. Here, I'd wanted for nothing.

Yet it had never felt like home.

Had Thomas and I ever been happy? I'd let myself believe we'd been content because I'd been stupid and blinded by material things. But none of this was mine.

The only thing I owned was my car. *Karson's* car.

"Will you miss it here?" Gemma asked.

I shook my head. "Not for a minute."

I'd gladly scrub my own toilets and mow my own grass for a chance to feel like a home was my own.

As a kid, I'd run away to be safe. I'd run away so I

wouldn't have to watch my parents implode. Slowly, I'd ventured east. I'd been searching for work and adventure. I'd found Thomas and he'd given me both, for a time.

Now, I was running away to find peace. To find the life I needed deep in my soul. To find myself again.

I'd lost *me* these past years. When I met Thomas, I was twenty-one. He was thirty-five.

We'd married when I was twenty-two, and he'd given me a job as his assistant. Thomas ran his own company in Boston and had made a fortune through corporate investments, capital endeavors and real estate trans-actions.

Working for him had been the first job I'd ever had that didn't pay minimum wage. I'd learned how to use a computer. I'd learned how to analyze spreadsheets and build presentations. At first, Thomas had taught me how to speak properly on the phone. Basically, I'd learned manners.

He'd taken all my rough edges and smoothed them away.

For the most part, I'd enjoyed the transformation to a cultured society wife. Once a kid who'd grown up in a single-wide trailer, eating processed cheese slices and SpaghettiOs from the can, I'd looked in the mirror and loved the shiny version of myself. I loved showering every day. I loved my expensive makeup and my monthly hair appointments.

The truth was, I would have kept on living this life,

turning a blind eye to the hole in my heart. But there were some things I refused to ignore.

Two years ago, Thomas had hired another assistant. He hadn't wanted to burn me out, even though I'd never complained about the work. I'd cut down to three days a week while she worked five.

We had different tasks, but we sat across from one another and would talk cordially as we worked. I'd take my lunch with Thomas in his office. Monday, Wednesday and Friday, he'd fuck me on his desk.

Apparently, Tuesday and Thursday were her days.

I'd walked in on them six months ago when I'd come into the office to surprise him for lunch.

This beautiful home and all the money in our checking account weren't worth the pain of a broken heart.

I grabbed my suitcase and wheeled it to the door. Gemma followed me outside, her heels clicking on the cement sidewalk as we walked to the detached garage beside the larger house. This garage wasn't where I parked normally. My BMW was in the garage, where Thomas parked his own Beemer. Maybe after I left, he'd give it to Secretary.

Fine by me. *My* car was parked here, where the gardener kept his tools.

I punched in the code to open the large door, the sun limning the space as it lifted. I walked in and ran my hand over the gray tarp that had covered the Cadillac for two years.

A rush of excitement hit as I peeled off the tarp. The chrome underneath gleamed as it caught the sun. The cherry-red paint was polished to a mirror shine.

"I still can't believe this is the same car." Gemma smiled from her position at the door.

"Remember that time when we sat in the back and smoked an entire pack of cigarettes?"

"Don't remind me." She grimaced. "I still can't stand the smell of smoke. I think I puked that entire night."

"We thought we were so tough at sixteen."

"We were."

We were. Along the years, we'd gotten soft. Maybe we'd used up all our tough to survive. Or maybe we'd forgotten how harsh the world could truly be.

"I wish I were tougher in here." I tapped my heart.

Her lip curled. "I hate him for this."

"Me too." I swallowed hard, not letting the emotions overwhelm me. Thomas had gotten all the tears he was going to get. "More than anything, I'm mad at myself. I should have known better. I should have seen him for who he truly was."

Loyalty wasn't a common theme in my life. I hadn't had it from my parents or the many strangers who'd drifted in and out over the years as temporary friends. I'd expected it from my husband.

"Fuck him."

"Fuck him." Gemma walked to the other side, helping me peel the tarp off the back and fold it into a square. Maybe the gardener could use it for something.

I opened the trunk of the car, the smell of metal and new upholstery wafting into the air. I smiled, taking in the wide space. I'd stowed a lot of things in the trunk once. I'd had it organized and sectioned to perfection. Food on the left side. Clothes and shoes on the right.

I retrieved my suitcase, wheeling it over and loading it in the trunk. "I guess I've come full circle. This was my closet once. Now it is again."

Gemma didn't laugh. "Please, be careful."

"It's only a road trip, Gemma." I slammed the trunk closed. "I'll be fine."

I walked to the driver's side, opened the door and slid into my seat. The leather scent chased away the stale air. The dash was fairly dust-free given how long this had been sitting unused. I ran my fingers over the smooth white steering wheel.

A 1964 Cadillac DeVille convertible. My pride and joy.

The passenger door opened with a pop and Gemma took her seat.

"Smells good, right?"

She smiled as she shut the door. "A lot better than when you and Karson lived here."

"Seems like a lifetime ago."

"It was." She ran her hand across the white leather seat—smooth as butter and smelling like money.

A lot of money. This car had been no more than rusted scrap when I'd paid to have it hauled from California to Boston. But I'd paid. Every dime put into this car was a dime I'd earned.

Thomas had made me sign a prenup when we'd gotten married. I'd been young and foolish. I hadn't countered a single term. What the hell had I known about contracts and legal documents?

I'd learned though. Working for his company had taught me a lot. As much as I hated how our marriage had ended, Thomas had given me something invaluable.

An education.

He'd helped me get my GED. Then he'd put me to work. And damn it, I'd worked my ass off. As his assistant, I didn't run to get his coffee or pick up dry cleaning. I proofread contracts. I built financial projections. I put together presentations for stakeholders and schmoozed potential investors with the best of them.

Thomas gave me rough ideas and projects. I added the polish.

Just like I'd done to this car.

I put the key in the ignition and turned, closing my eyes as the Cadillac rumbled to life. The smile on my face pinched my cheeks.

That glorious sound was my freedom.

I looked over at Gemma just in time to see her dab at

the corner of her eye. "No tears," I said. "This isn't goodbye."

"It feels like it," she whispered. "More than any of the other times, this feels like you won't be coming back."

I wasn't.

"Want to come with me?" I knew the answer but asked anyway.

"I wish I could but . . ." Gemma didn't need a new life.

"I'll drive you to your car." It was parked in the loop in front of the house, but I wanted these last few moments together. I put the Cadillac in drive and inched out of the garage.

The sunshine hit the metal hood. The tires rolled smooth on the driveway. Damn, it felt good to drive. Why had I let this thing sit for so long? The Cadillac had been finished for two years.

The Cadillac's restoration had taken nearly a year. When it was done, I'd driven it home and parked it in the garage. Besides the rare weekend when I took it out, the weekends Thomas was gone, it had mostly sat idle for two years. Two damn years because Thomas had insisted it would get ruined if I tried to drive this *boat* in city traffic every day.

I hadn't wanted to risk an accident, so I'd continued to drive the BMW, wearing my suits and heels. I'd played my part as the refined wife he'd gotten bored with.

All while the Cadillac sat, covered and alone.

Shame on me.

I'd hidden away something important in my life. I couldn't pin the blame on Thomas either, because I'd forgotten who I was.

Too soon, I inched up to Gemma's car and put the Cadillac in park. She didn't get out. Neither did I.

"I'll call," I promised.

"You better." She twisted to me and leaned over for one last hug.

We met in the middle. She gave me a tight squeeze and then she was gone, walking with grace and elegance to her car.

Gemma had grown up in a hovel worse than mine, but she'd always had this regal nature. She'd lived on her own since the tenth grade. She had no Ivy League education or family pedigree. Yet Gemma Lane was pure class.

I hit the button to lower the convertible's top, smiling wider as the summer air filled my nostrils along with the smell of fresh-cut grass and wind. "I love you, Gem."

"Love you, Lonny." She smiled, standing next to her Porsche. Then she raised a pointed finger at my nose. "Call me."

"I will." I laughed as she got in her car, slid on sunglasses and waved one last time before racing away.

The sound of her exit faded in the distance and I took a final quiet moment to look at the house I'd called home. The brown brick façade stood tall and stately. The arched double doors were traditional and fancy. The pillars bracketing the porch were pompous.

This house wasn't me.

But my car was.

I gripped the steering wheel with both hands. It hadn't always been white, just like the seats hadn't always been leather.

Had I gone too far with the restoration? Maybe Karson would feel like I'd butchered the thing. But deep in my heart, I believed this was what the car should have looked like in its glory days. This was how it should have been before someone had forgotten its beauty and left it in a junkyard for two teenagers to squat in for a couple of years.

The modern touches, like power windows and an air-ride suspension, were purely a comfort thing. I was glad for them, given I was about to drive across the country.

I hit the gas, speeding out of the loop. When I passed through the exterior gate, I took one final glance in the rearview mirror.

No more gates.

The traffic in the suburbs wasn't awful, but as I hit the city, things slowed to a crawl. It took an hour for the congestion to break, but break it finally did.

Then I raced.

Karson had always said running away from home was the best decision of his life. I had to agree.

The wind whipped through my hair as I sped along the highway. Just me and my cherry-red Cadillac.

On a runaway road.

CHAPTER TWO

Two days on the road and I was free.

Boston had been slowly suffocating me, something I hadn't realized until five hundred miles separated me from my former life.

Screw daily routines. Screw schedules. Screw structure and convention. I'd been trapped in normalcy and ignorant of the heaviness in my heart. Turning a blind eye to my problems had been easy with the schedule I'd maintained. Every minute of my life had been choreographed. Sitting idle hadn't held any appeal.

Now that I had time to think about why I'd kept myself so busy, I saw that routines and structure had become a necessary distraction. When I was working, running the house or organizing a function for Thomas's company, I didn't have time to think about the last time I'd truly smiled or laughed carefree. When I was spending time at the spa or shopping, I only relaxed enough to recharge my batteries. But the downtime had never been long enough to reflect.

Sitting behind the wheel of my car forced me to take a hard look at the past eight years.

When I'd started working for Thomas, I'd enjoyed the routine, mostly because it had been an anomaly. Knowing what each day would entail had been a new concept for me. Stability had been refreshing.

And I'd been blissfully in love with my husband. I'd fit our lives together—or fit my life to his.

Thomas required structure. He thrived on a schedule. The man knew what he was doing with precision, every single day for the upcoming three months mapped out in detail. Gemma was the same way. Maybe it was a CEO thing, but the two of them had next to no flexibility. No spontaneity.

Gemma, I understood. She was desperate for surety, and after our childhood, it made sense. But Thomas's motivation wasn't born from fear of the unknown or a chaotic youth. Thomas had discipline and drive in every aspect of his life because it made him money.

Success and status were Thomas's true loves.

Why had I tried so hard to fit that mold? Because of love? I'd convinced myself I was happy, but did I even know what *happy* was?

All questions I'd been asking myself since leaving

Boston. Maybe by the time I reached California, I'd have them answered.

In the meantime, I was shunning all structure. I took the road at my own pace, not worrying about the speed limit or keeping up with traffic. The clock on the dash meant nothing because I had nowhere to be.

It was peaceful, simply driving alone. When I'd made my way to Boston—and all the stops in between—it had been by bus. Trips since had been with Thomas, and if we hadn't been in an airplane, he'd been behind the wheel.

Maybe for the first time, I felt ultimate control.

No wonder Gemma had become a control freak. It was fucking awesome.

I'd plaited my hair in a tight braid, but the wind whipped a few strands free as the sun warmed my face. Occasionally, another vehicle would pass me by and the smell of gasoline would linger for a mile. Unless it was raining, I was driving with the top down.

The day I left Boston, I drove for five hours without even a bathroom break. I wanted to get the hell away from traffic and the city. Cutting through Connecticut and a sliver of New York, I didn't stop until I hit the middle of Pennsylvania.

I pulled off the interstate and found a midlevel motel. I checked in and slept for fourteen hours. The grueling months of the divorce, when Thomas had fought me hard to reconsider ending our marriage, caught up to me. So I recharged in my motel room, making up for the sleepless nights.

The next morning, I woke up tired, not ready to get on the road. So I didn't. What was the hurry? This journey had no deadlines.

I added another night to my stay and spent the day in bed with a box of pizza delivery and the television.

Thomas didn't have time for movies or binge-watching television shows. We'd had one television in the house, a flat screen in the informal dining area where we'd eat breakfast. Thomas turned it on to watch the news each morning over egg whites and turkey bacon.

I hadn't minded. Before I'd run away at sixteen, I'd spent countless hours in front of the TV. Nickelodeon and MTV had been my babysitters while my parents had been busy with their current drug of choice.

But now, when those memories weren't as sharp and TV didn't equate to loneliness, I found the mindless entertainment soothing.

I watched *John Wick* first, finally understanding the fuss about Keanu Reeves. I cried through *Beaches*, knowing I was lucky to have a similar friendship with Gemma. And I stayed up until three in the morning, laughing at a rom-com about bridesmaids.

The next morning, I slept in again, leaving before noon checkout. Then, instead of rushing for the road, I drove to a local café. For hours, somewhere in Pennsylvania, I sat at a window table watching traffic, eating lunch and eavesdropping on other conversations. I left long after the smell of the café's fresh pastries had seeped into my blond hair.

Even after driving for hours, the scent was still in my hair. I picked up a lock of it, bringing it to my nose to inhale the lingering yeast and sugar. I'd always been conscious of smells—mostly my own.

Was I spoiled? *Probably*. After sleeping in a rusted-out, junkyard Cadillac for two years, did I deserve to be a bit spoiled?

Maybe so.

One thing was for certain, running away was much easier with money, and for that, I was grateful.

I could pay for hotel rooms and café lunches. I would never fear the charge at a gas pump. I could stop for a decent meal in a sit-down restaurant instead of scraping together enough change for a dollar-menu cheeseburger.

The money I'd earned working had been considerable for a woman with a fresh GED and no higher education. A perk of being married to the boss. I'd saved it all, minus what I'd spent on the Cadillac. Everything else—our household budget, clothes, shoes, the spa, vacations—had been paid for by Thomas. I could live off my savings for years. Designer garb wasn't in my budget these days, but I'd had enough of labels to last a lifetime.

The interstate cut through the countryside and signs flew past every now and then. I reached for my purse, ready to dig for my phone and check a map.

"It's not there," I reminded myself. How long would it take to break that habit?

And I didn't need a map. I was on the East Coast and had to get to the West. How I traveled didn't need to be charted. I was driving. The road beneath my tires would take me there eventually.

A large truck roared past, its diesel exhaust leaving behind a black cloud. I scrunched up my nose and slowed, but the stink clung to the car. I'd been dealing with the same all afternoon.

"To hell with the interstate." I flipped my blinker at the next exit, seeing a sign for a gas station. I wanted to go a few miles without passing another car.

I refueled the Cadillac and washed the windshield. Then I went inside and bought a couple bottles of water and a bag of chips.

"Thanks," I said to the clerk. "I don't suppose you have a pay phone anywhere?"

"Sure do. Just go out the door and take a right. It's around the corner."

"Thanks again." I collected my things and took them to the car, dropping them in the open seat. Then I fished out some quarters from my purse and found the phone. It was old and the keys dirty. I pressed the black receiver to my ear and propped it against my shoulder as I dialed Gemma's number.

"Hello?"

"Hey, Gem." I smiled.

"Lonny?"

"Yes, it's me. See? I told you I'd call. I figured I'd get your voicemail."

She laughed. "Perfect timing. I'm in between meetings and alone for once. How's it going? Where are you?"

"Still in Pennsylvania, according to my receipt from the gas station. And it's good. I'm taking it slow."

"I figured you'd be across the Mississippi by now."

"Soon enough. How are you?"

"Fine." She blew out a long breath. "I miss you already."

"Miss you too." Though I was glad she'd declined my offer to come along. As much as a road trip would have been fun with my best friend, I needed to do this alone. This trip was for me.

"Listen, I need to tell you something. I hate to do it on your first call, but I don't want you calling Thomas."

I scoffed. "I hadn't planned on it."

"Good. Because he called me yesterday."

"What?" I tensed. "Why? What did he want?"

"To find you."

I rolled my eyes. "Well, tough shit."

"There's, uh . . . something else." She paused. "It's not good. Want me to tell you? Or not?"

Not. Whatever was happening with Thomas wasn't going to change anything. I wasn't going back.

He'd stifled me, something I was coming to realize the farther I got from Boston. He didn't care about my ideas or feelings because he was the business mogul and I was only the poor girl he'd turned into a princess.

He couldn't fathom I'd leave his riches because of *a silly office affair.*

No, I didn't want to know.

Gemma knew I didn't want anything to do with him. So why even bring up his call? Was Thomas sick or something? Was he hurt? Was he in trouble?

"Tell me." *Damn you, curiosity.*

"It's, um, Secretary."

I cringed. Neither Gemma nor I would speak the woman's name. That bitch had sat across from me for months, smiling and pretending to be a friend while secretly fucking my husband. Maybe he had actually fired her.

"She's pregnant."

The phone fell from my ear, the black plastic crashing into the wall beneath the booth. The cord swung back and forth like a man hanging from a noose. *Kind of like my marriage.*

Dead.

"Londyn!" Gemma's voice yelled into the phone, forcing me to pick it back up.

"I'm here." I cleared my throat. "That's what he called to tell you? Why?" Hadn't he hurt me enough? Why couldn't he leave me alone in my ignorance?

Gemma sighed. "He wanted you to know in case you decided to come back."

"I'll never come back." Not now.

"I'm sorry," Gemma whispered. "I shouldn't have told you."

"No, I'm glad you told me. I wanted to know. It doesn't change anything. Did he say anything else?"

"Only that he's worried about you."

"Well, he's got other things to worry about now." Like dealing with the doctor who'd performed his vasectomy. "I'm going to let you go. I'm sure you're busy."

"I shouldn't have told you," she muttered. "Will you call me again soon?"

"Sure." I didn't mean it as a lie, but it felt like one. I couldn't imagine not talking to Gemma, but one call and I'd been yanked back into the life I'd just left. Maybe temporarily cutting ties with her for a while would be best. I'd call again, just not as soon as she probably assumed.

"Take care of yourself," she said.

"Bye." I set the phone in its silver cradle.

There were two more quarters in my pocket, enough for another call. I stood staring at the keypad on the phone. Should I call Thomas? The urge to scream and yell bubbled up in my chest and my fingers brushed the phone.

Since the divorce, I hadn't gotten angry. I'd gone numb and stayed quiet. My lawyer had encouraged me to stay that way so he could get me the best settlement possible. Thomas and I might have had a prenup, but Thomas had still ended up paying.

I'd hired a really good lawyer.

Aside from my own savings, I'd taken ten million dollars away from my marriage in our divorce settlement. Every cent was now being used by an organization that supported runaway kids. That money paid for clothes and shelter. It paid for education and long-term housing.

Thomas had escalated my station in life. Now his money was doing the same for other unfortunate kids who needed a helping hand. That donation had eased the sting of the divorce. It had helped me keep my temper.

Until now.

Fuck him. I stepped away from the phone, my fists clenched and my teeth gritted.

Thomas didn't deserve fifty cents.

I turned away from the phone, practically jogging for the car. I pulled onto the road and drove past the on-ramp for the interstate. Raising my hand, I gave it the finger.

Fuck interstates. Fuck Secretary. Fuck husbands who got a vasectomy at thirty because they hadn't planned on getting married five years later.

I'd been the exception to Thomas's meticulously planned-out life. I'd been a spontaneous, lead-with-your-heart decision.

This baby was because he'd led with his dick.

Fuck him.

The yellow lines in the middle of the blacktop blurred as a sheen of tears coated my eyes. I slid on my sunglasses and blinked them away.

Miles and miles streaked past as I drove along the

quiet highway. The trees fencing the road were bright and tall under the June sky. Birds flew overhead. Occasionally a stream would appear, kissing the road before disappearing into the lush greenery.

It was picturesque and impossible not to appreciate.

The mental image of Thomas and Secretary holding a baby swaddled in pink was stuck in my head.

It was ironic that Thomas had impregnated the wrong woman. He'd begged and pleaded for me to stay, and if we'd had a baby, I wouldn't have left him. Betrayal or not, I would not have taken a child away from a life where he or she would have wanted for nothing.

But I didn't have a baby. I didn't have a family and probably never would.

The tears threatened again, but I refused to let them fall.

"No more," I whispered to myself. "He gets no more."

I had this adventure to give me purpose. I didn't need family when I had my freedom.

Holding tight to the steering wheel with one hand, I raised the other into the air. The moment my fingertips ascended above the windshield, they chilled. It was getting cooler now as the sun began its descent.

I'd crossed into West Virginia about an hour ago, a large, faded sign welcoming me to the state.

I stretched my hand higher, toward the fading light of the sky. Then I balanced the wheel with my knee, letting my other hand reach above. My arms stretched.

Freedom.

I was free. I was alone. I was lost.

And it was beautiful.

The air streamed through my fingers. As I stretched my arms higher, I filled my lungs, breathing deeper than I had in a long, long time.

I closed my eyes, for just a moment, until a lurch on my right tire sent the Cadillac jarring toward the centerline.

My eyes flew open, my hands snapped to the wheel. "Shit."

I yanked the wheel to get the car to my side of the road. I overcorrected. The Cadillac, the beast that she was, swayed and lurched again as the tires on the passenger side shook on the rumble strip.

Pop.

The right front corner of the car dropped. The Cadillac jerked to the side and I didn't have the strength to hold the wheel.

I hit the brake, too hard. Damn it! I was panicking and losing control. The *thwap* of my flat tire filled the air right before the screech of metal on metal. A guardrail was kind enough to stop me from dropping into a ditch.

The Cadillac came to a grinding stop. Dust billowed until the night breeze blew it away.

"Oh my God," I breathed. I was alive—if my heart didn't explode. My hands were fisted on the wheel, frozen, but the rest of my body was shaking. I couldn't seem to loosen my grip, so I left my hands white knuckled and let my head fall forward.

I closed my eyes, letting the adrenaline settle. When the shaking eased and my head stopped spinning, I let go of the steering wheel and pushed out of the car on unsteady legs.

With one hand on the car for balance, I made my way around the trunk to the other side.

"Shit." The Cadillac was smashed against the guardrail. There were streaks of red paint from where I'd dragged alongside it.

I hurried around the car again, this time to inspect the front. The tire was flat and the rim rested on the asphalt.

"No." I ran a hand through my hair. I must have hit a nail. The night was getting darker by the second, and though I could change a tire in the daylight, doing it at night was not a challenge I wanted to take on.

"This is why we have phones." I slammed my palm into my forehead. I should have bought a flip phone for emergencies. "Damn it."

And there wasn't a car in sight. I'd gotten my wish for a deserted road. How long had it been since I'd passed a town? I'd driven through a small town earlier but it had still been bright outside. It was at least an hour's drive behind me.

"Ahh!" I screamed to the sky. Not even the birds seemed to care. Which meant if I was kidnapped and murdered along this road, no one would be around to hear those screams either. "Fucking hell."

I stomped to the driver's seat and got in to put the convertible's top up. When it was secure, I collected my purse, slammed the door and popped the locks. Then I went to the trunk, digging into my suitcase for a pair of tennis shoes to trade out for my flip-flops.

"I should have stayed in Pennsylvania," I muttered as I set off down the road. I was hoping that another town or a house would appear if I kept on the path forward. There wasn't much behind me.

The farther I walked from the car, the further my stomach sank. That car was my safety blanket. Even in Boston, when it had been tucked away in the garage, I'd always known it was there, protected and safe.

Now it was on the highway, alone and vulnerable.

So was I.

I stole glances over my shoulder until it disappeared from my sight and I began counting steps to occupy my mind. When I got to five hundred, I was nervous. When I got to a thousand, I was so freaked out by the impending darkness, I stopped walking.

There was no sign of a town close. If there were homes nearby, they were hidden in the trees.

"This is crazy." I spun on a heel and ran to my car. I was sweating and out of breath when it came into view.

I ran faster.

When I reached the door, darkness had nearly

descended and I could hardly make out the handle. If I had walked another five hundred steps, I wouldn't have made it back before nightfall.

I collapsed into the driver's seat, locking myself inside as my heart pounded.

What had I been thinking? Why would I leave this car? I'd sleep here tonight and flag down a passing car tomorrow. Because I wasn't leaving this car again. The only time we'd part ways was when I handed the keys to Karson in California.

If he was even in California. I'd find out when I got there.

The air was thick and humid outside my window. Sweat ran down my cleavage and soaked the hair around my temples and forehead. I turned on the car, cranking up the AC until I wasn't dripping. Then I cracked the windows and shut it off, pushing my seat back as far as it would go to stretch out my legs.

Sleeping in the Cadillac was more comfortable in the backseat, something I knew from years of practice, but sleep wouldn't come easy tonight no matter where I rested. And from here, I could see outside better and hop out quickly if a car approached.

Hours passed. Stars lit up the midnight sky. Thousands of them hovered overhead, and like I'd done as a teenager, I wished on the brightest. Lost in their random pattern, I jumped when a flash of light caught my eye from the rearview mirror.

I sat up, spinning around as blinding headlights raced my way. I flew into action, turning on the Cadillac's interior light before getting out. I hurried to stand by the hood, inching back until the guardrail brushed my calves. Then I waved my arms in the air like a lunatic as the other vehicle approached.

I squinted at their headlights, using one hand to shield my eyes as the other waved. The car didn't slow. The hum of its engine seemed to grow louder. Did they not see me? Or were they going to pass me by?

My stomach dropped as the lights got closer and closer with no sign the vehicle was slowing. My arm was still raised in the air but I'd stopped waving.

They were going to keep driving. *Asshole.*

Given my luck today, that was about par for the course. I was ready to give them the finger too when tires squealed and the engine's loud downshift filled the air.

"Thank you," I breathed, dropping my hand.

A truck came to an abrupt stop right beside me, and the window lowered. My eyes were still filled with spots from the headlights, but I squinted hard, trying to make out the driver.

"Need some help?"

It was a woman's voice. *Thank you, stars.* One of my wishes was to be rescued. Another was for my rescuer to be female.

I stepped closer to the truck. "I have a flat and am squished into the guardrail. It's dark and I didn't want to try and change it myself. And . . ." I sighed. "I don't have a phone."

"Damn." She stretched the word across two syllables. *Day-um.* "Well, Summers is about ten miles up the road. Want a lift?"

Ten miles? I was glad I'd turned around. "Is there a tow truck in Summers? I'd rather not leave my car out here."

"Cohen's got a tow. Want me to call him?"

"Yes, please. Thank you so much." My eyes were finally adjusting to the dark. As she took out her phone, the screen illuminated the cab briefly, and I was able to see her face.

The woman was likely in her late fifties, but with the dim light, it was hard to tell. The wrinkles around her eyes and mouth were slight. Her hair was either a light blond or gray. She pressed the phone to her ear and faced me, giving me a kind smile.

Of all the people in the world who might have stopped, I'd hit the jackpot. I stepped closer until I was standing right outside the open passenger window. The scent of lemon bars wafted from the truck and filled my nose.

My stomach rumbled. The chips I'd inhaled hours ago had long since burned away.

"Hey, Brooks." She didn't introduce herself to the person on the other end of the phone. "I've got a gal here who needs a tow. About ten miles north of town, a mile or so before you hit my place."

Her place? So if I'd gone the other direction, I'd have landed myself at her house? *Damn it.* From now on, I was paying better attention to my surroundings as I drove. This wouldn't have happened if I hadn't been trying to work myself out of a funk.

"Sure thing." She hung up, setting her phone in the console. "He's on his way."

"Thank you." Would it be weird to give her a hug?

"Want me to wait with you, sweetheart?"

My heart warmed. "No, you go ahead. Thank you."

"It's late. I'm on my way to the motel to deliver some lemon bars to my sister, Meggie. I bake when I can't sleep and she works the evening and night shifts. You come on over after Brooks gets you and that car to town. Stay the night in Summers."

"I think I'll do that. Thank you."

"Good. My name's Sally. And you are?"

"Londyn McCormack."

"Fine meeting you, Londyn." She lifted a hand. "See you soon."

I waved, stepping away from her truck as she put it in drive. As quickly as she'd come to a stop, she was off, racing down the highway and leaving me in the dark.

I got back in my car, swatting at the bugs that had latched on to my skin and hitchhiked their way into the car. Then I waited, watching the clock as ten minutes ticked by. Then fifteen. At twenty, I was starting to wish I'd hitched a ride with Sally after all, but then two headlights came around a bend.

I got out and waited in my same spot by the hood, only this time, my own headlights were shining too.

The tow truck came to a slow stop, the engine running as the driver opened the door and stepped onto the road. His dark, tall figure was shadowed as he walked through the streaming light.

"Ma'am." His hand lifted as he stepped close and his features came into view. "Heard you needed a tow."

I swallowed hard. Was I asleep? I had to be asleep. Sally was a dream and so was he. I had no experience with tow truck drivers but surely this wasn't what they all looked like. Otherwise the women of the world would be constantly popping their tires.

He shifted, blocking out more of the light with his broad shoulders. The move gave me a clearer view of his face and highlighted the line of his straight nose. Stubble dusted his strong jaw. His arms were roped with muscles so defined I wouldn't be surprised if he picked up my car with his bare hands to set it on the tow's flatbed.

"Ma'am?"

"Yes." I blinked, forcing my gaze away from his soft lips to return his handshake. "Sorry. I, uh . . . have a flat and can't change it."

"Hmm." He walked to the car, peering down the side

pressed against the guardrail. "Looks like you got more than a flat."

My eyes drifted to the man's ass. *Day-um.* As he turned, I forced my eyes to his face. The last thing I needed was for him to leave me on the side of this road. "I scraped against the guardrail as I skidded to a stop. I don't even want to think about what the side of my car looks like."

"Probably not pretty. But we'll get it to the garage and take a closer look."

"Thanks." I smiled. "I appreciate you coming out here so late to help me."

He chuckled. "When Sally calls, it's best you answer, ma'am."

I cringed at the third ma'am. "It's Londyn. Spelled with a y."

"Londyn. Pleasure." Oh lord, that voice, so rich and smooth. I hoped his name was something plain like George or Frank. Something to combat the perfection. "I'm Brooks Cohen."

Not George. This was definitely a dream.

CHAPTER THREE

BROOKS

Tonight wasn't the first time I'd gotten a tow call from Sally Leaf well after midnight. Normally, she needed me to tow her out of whatever ditch she'd managed to drop her old truck into. The woman drove like speed limits were a minimum and lines on the highway a suggestion.

Regardless, whenever she called, I came running. I'd hauled my ass out of my bed, then dressed in jeans and a T-shirt. I'd hurried the few blocks from my house to the garage, where I'd swapped out my silver Ford for the tow rig. As Sally had promised, almost exactly ten miles out of town, I'd spotted the car sandwiched against the guardrail.

A gorgeous car. And a goddamn knockout owner.

Londyn. *Spelled with a y.*

Her Cadillac was loaded onto the flatbed and she was riding shotgun with a purse clutched in her lap. The sweet scent of her hair drifted my way each time she made the slightest movement to shift her handbag or cross her legs.

Thank goodness it was dark and she couldn't see my wandering eyes. They'd skimmed her from head to toe, taking in that long blond hair as it draped over her shoulders and the swells of her breasts. Her loose jeans couldn't hide the rounded contours of her hips or the firm lines of her legs.

My mother would be ashamed to know I'd checked out her ass more than once.

I ducked my head, sneaking a quick sniff of my arm. *Oh, hell.* I smelled like sweat and grease. I'd showered before bed, washing away a day of grime from the garage and the stink of the five miles I'd run after work. But after loading up her car in the sticky heat, I'd melted right through my quick swipe of deodorant.

"You just passing through?" I asked as I rolled the window down a few inches. I knew the answer to that question. If she lived around here, I'd know it. Summers was my hometown and I'd lived here all my life. After thirty-three years, there weren't many people I didn't know. But we'd ridden two miles in uncomfortable silence, and I was desperate to ease the tension.

"Yes. I'm on my way to California."

"From?"

"Boston."

I whistled. "That's a long trip."

And a dangerous one for a woman on her own. I didn't

36

like to think about what might have happened had she gotten a flat somewhere other than outside Summers, West Virginia.

"I'm in no hurry." She sighed, toying with the strap on her purse.

I sat a little straighter, pretending to glance at the car in the rearview, instead checking my face. My hair was a goddamn mess. I ran a hand through it twice, taming down the dark blond sticking up on top.

Shit. When was the last time I'd cared about my hair?

"Where are you taking my car?" she asked.

"To my garage. I'll take a closer look at it tomorrow, but when I loaded it up, I saw some damage to the wheel. The side panel's pretty banged up too."

"Damn it," she grumbled, dropping her head into her hand. "I can't believe I did this."

"Accidents happen." They were never expected and never convenient.

"This one shouldn't have," she muttered. "I don't suppose you do any custom car work? I had the entire thing restored and need to get it fixed."

"I've done some." More than some, but I wasn't going to promise I could fix her Cadillac until I got a better look at the damage. "Like I said, let's see what we're dealing with tomorrow."

"Okay." She leaned against the door, her frame slumped. She looked like she was about five minutes from falling asleep.

"Where you staying?"

"Sally mentioned something about a motel."

"I'll drop you there, then take your car to the shop."

She hummed her agreement as we reached the edge of town. I slowed as the highway turned into Main Street, then veered off to park in front of the Summers Motel.

There were fifteen rooms in total, all situated in a horseshoe around an office in the center. Guests mostly parked in the loop, but the tow truck was too large for the space so I stopped us along the sidewalk.

As expected, Sally's truck, dented and dinged, was parked beside the office. Inside, she was laughing with her twin sister, Meggie. The two were eating something, probably a dessert of sorts. Sally was always experimenting with cookies and cakes. Those two would load themselves up on sugar for a few hours and chase it down with a gallon of coffee.

No surprise that Sally was rarely seen in town before noon. Meggie owned the motel and had worked the night shift for as long as I could remember. She said it was so her employees could have the normal hours. My theory was that she and Sally were born night owls.

"Here we are."

Londyn looked over, giving me a hint of a smile. "Thank you. I'll come by the garage tomorrow."

"No rush. It'll take me some time to figure out what we're dealing with here. I can call you if you'd like. Tell you when to come down."

"Okay—no, wait," she grumbled. "I don't have a phone."

"You don't have a phone?"

"No."

My jaw dropped. "You're driving across the country without a phone? Ma'am, I know I just met you. But it's—"

"Not safe. I'm aware."

I opened my mouth, a lecture ready, but stopped myself. For now, she'd be at the motel and I could reach her here. Besides, she wasn't my concern. This woman was a stranger. She'd be out of Summers the minute her car was ready. So why did the idea of her traveling alone leave me with such an unsettled feeling in my gut?

"I'll call the motel in the morning. The garage is about three blocks away. You feel like taking a walk before I call, come on down."

"Okay." She nodded, opening her door to step down.

I unbuckled and jumped out of the rig, rounding the front to make sure she made it to the ground from the tall step. "I got the door."

"Thanks." She tucked a lock of hair behind her ear as I stepped close to slam the door behind her. "See you tomorrow."

I followed her to the sidewalk. "Have a good night."

Londyn waved but stopped midstep, gesturing to the Cadillac. "All my things are in the trunk."

"That's no problem." I walked to the flatbed and vaulted up. "Toss me your keys."

She dug them out of her purse, but instead of throwing them over, she lifted one of those long legs and hopped right up next to me. "I got it."

We shuffled to the back, where she popped the trunk. It was packed with two suitcases and a matching duffel bag. The print matched her purse too. My mom had the same luggage, something Dad had bought her for an anniversary gift last year.

That was not a cheap print. Given that her car was worth twice as much as mine, I wasn't surprised she had designer bags too.

She went to take a suitcase out, but I took it from her grip. The slight brush of her fingers against mine was like a firebolt running up my hand. Londyn froze, her eyes widening and cheeks flushing. A surge of heat ran through my blood.

Who was this beautiful woman?

Londyn broke eye contact first, dropping her gaze to the trunk. I hoisted out the backpack and strung it over a shoulder. Then I pulled out both suitcases, setting them on the flatbed as she locked up the trunk.

I hopped down first, holding out a hand to help Londyn. She took it, this second touch as electric as the first.

Goddamn. I was in trouble if it took more than a day or two to get her car on the road. I let her go and reached for the suitcases.

"I can get them," she offered.

"Sally and Meggie would have my hide if I didn't carry in your bags." Then they'd call my mother and she'd deliver her own licking.

I led the way to the motel, setting aside the luggage to open the door for her. Sally was off her stool and rushing to greet Londyn.

Sally swallowed a bite of whatever she'd been chewing. "Come on in here, sweetheart."

"I've got your room all ready," Meggie said. "Room five."

Sally winked. "It's the best one."

"You're in good hands. I'll see you tomorrow." I deposited Londyn's bags and waved goodbye. "Night, ladies."

A chorus of good nights followed me into the dark.

"Heavens, that man has an ass that won't quit."

I chuckled, rolling my eyes at Meggie's comment. She was twenty-something years my senior and had made it her personal mission in life to make sure I knew she appreciated my body.

I took one last look at the lobby as I climbed into the truck. Londyn's eyes shot up from where she'd been staring at my ass.

I grinned. I guess we were even now.

———

"MORNING, BR—" Tony looked me up and down. "There a funeral or wedding I didn't hear about?"

"No." I shrugged. "I needed a cut and shave."

"Look awful slick for a man who was up half the night towing in this car." He tapped a knuckle on the hood of Londyn's red Cadillac. "She must be prettier than Sally let on."

"I don't know what you're talking about."

"Uh-huh," he muttered, his chest shaking with a silent laugh.

Sally and Tony had been lovers for more years than I'd been alive. They weren't married. They lived in separate homes. But when she finally retired to bed, it was usually in his. That, or he was already asleep in hers. They didn't date other people. They'd been blissfully *single* for decades but were the farthest thing from it.

Sally had probably woken up early with Tony this morning—or hadn't even gone to bed yet—to give him all the details on Londyn.

She was pretty. Damn pretty. I doubted anything Sally could say would do Londyn justice. But I hadn't stopped at the barbershop *only* for Londyn. It was summer and too hot for a mop on my head and scruff on my face.

"Just needed a shave, Tony."

"Whatever you say, boss."

I ignored his smirk and walked around to the damaged side of the Cadillac, crouching down on the concrete to get a closer look.

"She did a number on this panel." My fingers skimmed the scratches that led from the passenger door to the back taillight. "The front tire's shot too."

It had to be more than a nail to blow out one of these tires. They were a custom size and practically new. Some might try to save a buck and fix this one, but it wouldn't be a solid repair.

Londyn's safety had crept up my list of priorities awfully fast.

"I'll order a new tire first thing. Get it fixed today."

"What about the panel?" Tony asked, sipping from a steaming mug of coffee. I'd never understand how he could drink it boiling hot all day long, even when it was a hundred degrees outside and the humidity was off the charts.

"I'll get ahold of Mack at the body shop. If I get this tire fixed today, maybe he can fit it into his schedule this week to fix the paint."

Which meant Londyn would be on her way in three or four days and I wouldn't feel the need to keep going to the barbershop at seven in the morning for a shave and a haircut.

"Hello?" A soft, silky voice filled the shop and made my pulse race.

"Morning, miss." Tony grinned. "How can we help you?"

I stood, catching up to him before he could shake

Londyn's hand with his greasy palm. I clapped him on the shoulder. "I got this, Tony."

He looked at me, then at Londyn and back again. A slow grin spread across his cheeks, revealing the dimples that Sally praised as often as Meggie did my ass. "Then I think I'll take a wander down the road to see what kind of treats the Express Hut has today and get a refill on my coffee."

Tony bowed a bit as he passed Londyn, twisting his wrist in a wave.

I waited until he was out of earshot, then tipped my head to Londyn. "Mornin'. How was the rest of your night?"

"It was fine. Uneventful. I just fell asleep."

I did my best not to think of Londyn anywhere near the vicinity of a bed, but it was difficult given her attire. She wore a pair of shorts that molded to the perfect curve of her hips. The V-neck of her tee plunged to reveal a delicious line of cleavage.

"Brooks?"

Fuck. She'd caught me staring at her breasts. I spun away from her, running a hand through my fresh haircut. "So, uh . . . the car."

"I was anxious to see it in the light of day so I didn't wait for you to call. How bad is it?" She walked deeper into the garage, her flip-flops slapping with each step. If I'd offended her, she didn't let on. Her focus was entirely on the Cadillac.

"It's not horrible." I went to the wrecked side. "I'm going to get the wheel fixed today, but I think a patch won't last to California. It'll be best to buy a new tire."

"Okay. And the side?"

"The panel has a few minor dents but nothing that can't be popped out. The paint will have to be touched up."

"And you can do all that?"

"I'm more of an engine guy. I fix a lot of tires for folks in town. Body work isn't my specialty."

I'd make a mess of this kind of precision work, and I could tell someone had dumped a ton of money into this car. This Cadillac had all the modern touches to the interior and the engine was top of the line. When I'd unloaded it off the tow truck last night, I hadn't been able to resist a look under the hood.

The engine was almost as sexy as the woman at my side.

Almost.

"I don't know what this car looked like in the before picture, but I'm guessing it was a complete rebuild, right?"

"Yes. I had it restored a couple of years ago."

"Had to have been expensive."

"It wasn't cheap, let's just say that."

I chuckled. "Figured as much."

"What do I do? I'd really like to avoid having to go back to Boston to get it fixed. And I can't take it to California as it is. Shit." Before I could help, she started

45

pacing, running her hands through the ponytail that hung over one shoulder. "I should have stayed on the interstate."

"Why'd you get off?"

She lifted a shoulder. "I was tired of being on that road."

I had a feeling she wasn't talking about the pavement.

"The interstate is overrated." I looked down at her, studying the color of her eyes.

They were a rich green close to the shade of a dark jade ring my sister had bought on a visit to Asia last year. Though Londyn's eyes were far more beautiful and unique than that simple stone. I suspected a lot about her story was one of a kind.

"I've got a good friend who owns a body shop in town. He's good. He can get the dents worked out and the paint redone on this side. He's usually booked out months, but he owes me a favor because I rebuilt an engine for him last year. I'll call it in."

"Thank you." She blew out a long breath. "How long?"

"Three or four days. That going to be a problem?"

"No, I guess not." She turned to the open door of the garage, looking past the large sycamore that towered over the parking lot. "I guess I'll have some time to explore Summers."

"It's a nice town. There are likely worse places to be stranded."

"Probably." She smiled. "I walked over this morning and from the bit I've seen, it does seem nice."

"The diner has the best pie in West Virginia."

"Is that right?" She raised an eyebrow. "I guess I'll have to try it out."

"Their cheeseburgers aren't bad either."

"Good to know. So you'll call me?"

I nodded, then dug into my jeans pocket to retrieve a small black flip phone. "Here."

She eyed it. "What's that?"

"A cheap phone from Walmart."

Her eyes snapped to mine and as they caught the overhead light, flecks of caramel glinted in the center starburst. Beautiful, like everything else about this mysterious woman.

"Here." I held it out.

She didn't take it. "You got me a phone?"

"I did."

"Why?"

Because last night I'd tossed and turned, thinking of her on the side of the highway, stranded and alone. "You're a single woman traveling by yourself. You should have a phone."

"Thanks, but no, thanks."

I stepped closer. "I don't want to turn on the news one night to see a story about how that gorgeous woman whose car I helped fix got butchered by some maniac at a rest stop outside California."

Her cheeks flushed. "Gorgeous?"

"You've got a mirror, Londyn." Of course she'd caught the one word I hadn't meant to say. But it was out there now and I'd own the slip. It was the damn truth.

She blushed, a smile toying at the corners of her mouth as she stared at the phone. "You don't even know me. Why do you care?"

"Just the kind of man I am, so do me a solid. Cut me a break and take the phone. My number's in the texts."

She picked it up from my palm, opening it only to close it immediately. "Three days?"

"Maybe four. Then you'll be on your way."

And I'd always wonder what had happened to the woman with the jade-green eyes and hair the color of a wheat field in fall. Had she made it to California? Had she turned back for Boston?

Maybe in five years, I'd dial the number to that phone just to see where Londyn had landed.

Maybe she'd even answer.

CHAPTER FOUR

LONDYN

Summers, West Virginia.

The little town surprised me. I'd awoken this morning expecting to feel restless and impatient to leave. My journey to California was in its infancy and being stranded should have made me feel twitchy. On the contrary, I was actually enjoying myself.

There was something about this place. Something different than anywhere else I'd visited or lived. Charm, maybe? Everydayness? I couldn't put a word to it, but whatever the feeling, it had wrapped around me like a warm blanket. Yet again, maybe that was just the humidity.

As I walked down a quiet road, my soul was at peace. I wasn't panicked or worried about my car's repairs. I trusted Brooks to set the Cadillac to rights—another surprise, considering I'd only just met the man.

My steps were easy and slow as I strolled, my attention on the towering trees. This town had more trees than anywhere else I'd visited. Not a lawn I passed had less than two shading the green grass. Their canopy created a pocket in the world, the towering branches shedding glitter as sunlight broke through the leaves to illuminate the pollen floating to the ground.

It was easy to think the rest of the world didn't exist in this cocoon. I'd found a long residential street on my explorations this morning. It was straight as an arrow and the trees arched over the blocks. It was like stepping into a wardrobe and finding Narnia—minus the ice queen. There was no flat tire. There was no ex-husband or pregnant mistress. Of all the places in the world to get stuck, Summers was now at the top of my list.

"Morning." A man on a porch raised a hand.

"Good morning." I smiled, replaying the words with his Appalachian accent.

I hadn't heard it before coming to Summers, and even here, not many had it. The inflections were different than a Southern drawl. Those who spoke with the accent barely seemed to move their lips as they talked.

The man nodded from his rocking chair on the porch as I passed, his newspaper in hand. He looked comfortable there, like he might sit out all day. Or maybe he'd duck inside soon to the air conditioning. It was midmorning and the heat was on the rise. Coupled with the humidity, it was like breathing air from a steam room.

By the time I went to bed tonight, I'd likely be a sticky mess.

Why didn't that bother me? Another wonder. I liked the thick air. My skin felt supple and my lungs hydrated. There were days in Boston when the summer was sweltering and muggy. I'd come home from work and dive into the shower to rinse off the grime and sweat. This air, while heavy, had a sweet and earthy smell like flowers blooming and tree bark. Nature's perfume, untainted by exhaust and city waste.

My flip-flops slapped on the concrete sidewalk as I meandered past yellow homes and white homes and green homes. Not a single house on the block was the same color. Each had its own character and intricate details to set it apart from its neighbors. One owner had covered their lawn with garden gnomes. Another had painted the front door a perky teal.

This was the slowest I'd walked in years, soaking it all in.

Maybe someday I'd come back and see if this street was the same. I'd visit this place in the fall to see the leaves as they changed from green to red, orange and yellow. Maybe I'd see if Brooks Cohen was just as handsome then as he was now.

But I didn't need to revisit Summers to satisfy that curiosity. Brooks was the type of man who only grew more handsome with age. I was guessing he was in his early thirties. His body was solid and even if it softened some, he'd always be drool-worthy. With a few gray streaks in his blond hair, he'd be irresistible.

I'd always had a thing for older men.

A shrink would probably chalk it up to daddy issues. I think it was because I'd grown up fast—too fast. Men my own age always seemed to lag behind.

Brooks wore his maturity with confidence. He put on no pretense. He was simply . . . himself. He didn't seem defined by his occupation or his clothes. He was magnetic in a plain white T-shirt and a well-worn pair of jeans.

That thin cotton T-shirt had stuck to Brooks when he'd rescued me on the side of the road. It had molded to his sturdy arms and rugged chest as he'd moved around the Cadillac. The muscles on his back were so well defined, I'd fought the urge to skim my fingertips down his shoulders just to feel the dents and contours under my skin.

A shiver ran down my spine.

He was a fantasy.

I didn't let myself indulge in fantasies often. Hope was something I kept at a firm distance. Disappointment, on the other hand, was a close companion.

With Brooks, I let the fantasy play out. I was in Summers for a hot minute, not enough time for him to crush the illusion in those strong, firm hands.

God, I wanted those hands on me. My core clenched and my nipples hardened inside my bra. Was he married? I hadn't seen a ring but maybe he didn't wear one. Did he have a girlfriend?

I didn't feel right lusting after another woman's man, so in my fantasy, he was single unless and until disappointment reared its evil head and smothered this fantasy too.

Brooks had consumed my thoughts all night long. His T-shirt had been the star of my dreams, the way it would stretch as it was dragged up that sticky body. I'd slept with a pillow between my legs just for some friction to calm the ache.

"I need sex," I muttered to myself.

I needed a good, hard fuck and a long, sweaty night. I needed an orgasm that didn't come from my own fingers or the showerhead. I needed to have a man's weight on top of me as he pressed me into a bed.

When was the last time I'd had sex in a bed?

More than a year. Thomas and I hadn't had a great sex life at home. In the office, we were great, but not at home. I should have known something was up when he always wanted to fuck me on his desk. Had he been picturing Secretary in my place?

Does it matter?

The truth was, Thomas and I hadn't been in love. I'd respected him. I'd admired him. I'd adored him. But love? I wasn't sure. Did I even know how it felt to be in love?

I'd thought so, but I was questioning everything these days. Could a woman who'd grown up without affection or care really know what it was to be in love?

Maybe I'd mistaken attention for love.

I was jonesing for some physical attention. A hookup

would not go unappreciated. Maybe Brooks Cohen would do me a favor before I rolled out of town. If he wasn't attached, he'd be the perfect candidate to break my dry spell.

In a goddamn bed.

My hunch was that Brooks was a considerate lover. A gentleman. He'd called me ma'am and tipped his invisible hat when he'd dropped me off at the motel. I was probably reading too much into it, but I sure would like to be with a man who knew a woman's pleasure came first.

The street came to an end before I was ready to leave my West Virginian Narnia and I paused at the stop sign, tempted to walk it again. But the temperature was rising and I could use a cold glass of water, so I took a right and carried onward.

I wasn't sure how long I'd been out walking. The phone Brooks had bought me was tucked into the pocket of my jean shorts, but on principle, I hadn't turned it on.

I didn't need a phone. I didn't want a phone. But he'd worn me down.

Just the kind of man I am.

I wasn't carrying this phone for me. I had it in my pocket for Brooks.

His simple explanation might not mean a lot for women who'd grown up with decent men in their lives. But for me, a good man was as elusive as presents on Christmas morning.

So I'd taken the phone and kept it close.

Brooks Cohen. Damn, I liked him. I liked the entire package, head to toe. Even his unique name gave me a shudder.

The one thing my parents had done right was to give me a cool name. My mother had named me Londyn after the city in England because she'd always wanted to visit there. The woman couldn't spell for shit.

Unfortunately, by the time I'd run away at sixteen, I'd picked up her spelling habits. Mom didn't write much—she didn't need to as a lifelong junkie—but when I'd been eight, I'd taken over responsibility for going to the grocery store around the block.

Wanting the escape, I went almost every day, and because my scrawny arms couldn't carry more than three bags home. Mom would send me with a tattered sticky note covered in her messy script with words spelled entirely wrong.

Melk. Bred. Sereel.

The few teachers I'd had in my early years had tried to correct my spelling. Some had succeeded. Others hadn't cared. But I'd gotten by. Who needed to spell when you worked at bars and understood your own notes?

I hadn't seen it as a flaw until I'd married Thomas.

I'd never forget the look on his face when he'd seen my GED study notes. It was one of the most humiliating moments in my life. He'd stared at me like I was a broken child, not an adult, a grown woman and his *wife.*

From then on out, I took care to double-check every

single word before writing it down. I'd spent hours with a dictionary in hand. I still carried a pocket version in my purse. Math, science and world history would never be my forte, but damn it, I could spell. And my vocabulary wouldn't betray my upbringing.

After another two blocks, I changed direction for the motel, hot and ready for an iced coffee. Meggie had set up a small coffee area in the motel's office, and this morning, all of the chairs had been filled with locals. Gossip flew from one end of the reception area to the other. Some bounced to the counter, where the clerk whipped up coffee and kept watch over the covered cake stand.

Free, black coffee was available to anyone who came through the door. Fancy espressos and the treats under the glass dome were for paying customers only. The scone I'd inhaled this morning rivaled any I'd found at my favorite patisserie in Boston.

At the next intersection, I stopped and looked both ways, getting my bearings. Then I took a left, hoping I'd come up on the back side of Main Street. When the sound of an air gun filled the air, I tensed.

It was a sound often heard in a garage—a squeak and a puff of air with a compressor churning. Whenever my mechanic in Boston had called to talk about the Cadillac, that sound had been a constant in the background.

Somehow, I'd gotten turned around and ended up behind Brooks's garage.

I slowed, contemplating a retreat. I didn't want Brooks

to think I was hovering. Though I did want to see my car and find out what was happening. That wasn't weird, was it? I was in the area. A brief stop in wasn't hovering, even if I'd been over yesterday.

Plus I'd get to see the mechanic himself. I wasn't going to be in Summers long. I might as well add fodder for my future fantasies while I had the chance. Maybe today, Brooks would be in a different color T-shirt.

Decision made, I walked to the large open door and peeked my head inside. This wasn't a large garage. There were only two stalls and a small office in the back corner. The tow truck was parked alongside the building in a gravel lot.

"Um . . ." I raised my hand to knock, except there was no place to knock, so I awkwardly tucked it away. "Hello?"

My car was in the same place it had been yesterday. The tire was no longer flat. Beside it in the next bay was a minivan raised in the air on a hoist. Tools were strewn on workbenches. The scent of grease hung in the air.

Not a soul was visible.

Which was probably for the best. Now that I was standing in the middle of the doorway, this seemed more like stalker than concerned customer. I spun around, hoping to make a quick escape, but a deep, sexy voice stopped my retreat.

"Londyn."

I froze. *Shit.*

"Uh, hi." I waved, turning around as Brooks came

striding out of the office. "I was just walking around town. I passed by and thought I'd come to check on my car."

That didn't come across as stalking but it sure sounded a lot like I didn't trust him at all to do his job.

"Car's fine." He grinned. "Still alive."

I blushed. My hand was in the air so I pulled it down, tucking it away. Then we stood there, him staring at me while I looked around the room. Why was this awkward?

Oh, right, because he was gorgeous and somehow I'd forgotten how to speak to gorgeous men. Or because I couldn't stop thinking about stripping him of that T-shirt. Today, Brooks had traded his white T-shirt for a black one with a round crest printed on the center.

Cohen's Garage. The logo was made out of a gear. It was vintage in the way that it had once been a modern design—meaning, actually vintage. The short sleeves banded tight around his biceps, showing off the definition between shoulder and triceps. The cotton stretched across his pecs. I'd never fawned over a T-shirt so hard in my life. What I really wanted was to see it tossed on the floor of my motel room.

Another rush of desire pooled in my lower belly and the flush in my cheeks burned hotter. I was drooling. And staring.

You're staring.

"I'm going to go." I spun on a heel and marched away from the garage. The heat of desire shifted to the scorching flame of humiliation. *Jesus.* I was such a mess. His gaze burned into my backside as I scurried. There was no doubt he thought I was a lunatic.

"Got that phone?" Brooks hollered after me.

I pulled it from my pocket, holding it high in the air.

His chuckle followed me out of the parking lot.

AFTER THE DISASTROUS stop at the garage, I hid in my motel room for the remainder of the day.

I turned on the TV, doing my best to get lost in another movie, but unlike the Pennsylvania hotel where I'd struck movie rerun gold, nothing caught my attention.

Not trusting myself to inadvertently wander back to Cohen's Garage, I stayed within the confines of my room until my stomach growled and I went in search of food. My first stop was the office, hoping I'd find a restaurant or two willing to deliver.

"Hi, Londyn." Meggie smiled as I walked through the door, the bell dinging over my head.

"Hi, Meggie. Do you have any places in town that would deliver dinner? I walked all over this morning and I'm worn out."

Today's miles in bad shoes had been a harder workout than I'd anticipated. Maybe because I was so out of shape. In Boston, I'd been religious about the gym up until I'd found Thomas with Secretary. I didn't need glutes of steel or a flat stomach when the only person who saw me naked was *me*.

That, and I really liked delivery. I'd never bothered learning how to cook.

"Sure do." Meggie opened a drawer and lifted out a stack of menus.

I raised my eyebrows as she fanned them on the counter. "More options than I would have expected in Summers."

"If I could make a recommendation, how do you feel about Thai food? The place here makes the best curry you've had in your life."

"I could eat curry."

"I was hoping you'd say that." She smiled, picking up the phone. "If their delivery driver is coming, I might as well place an order myself."

Meggie got on the phone, not even introducing herself before placing the order. I guess whoever she was calling knew it was her or had seen the motel's number come up. I gave her cash for my part of the order and she took care of the rest.

As she talked, I paced around the reception area. All of the chairs were empty now, the locals who'd come in for coffee having gone home while I'd been in hiding.

The stretch in my legs was welcome after lying around all afternoon. I probably could have explored and found a dinner spot, but while I assumed Summers was a safe place, I didn't go out on foot at night.

Habits and all.

After running away from home, I'd spent a few dark nights wandering alone. I'd never felt such crippling fear as those times. Nothing had happened to me, thankfully, but the fear had been paralyzing enough.

It had nearly driven me home. The fact that it hadn't, well . . . it spoke of how bad things really had been with my parents. Once I'd found the junkyard, I'd made it a point to always be inside before dark. If I was working late, Karson would escort me home.

To the Cadillac.

"Should be here in thirty," Meggie said, the phone clicking onto the receiver.

"Thanks. You must be starving." She'd ordered two plates of curry for herself and one for me. Or maybe their serving portions were small.

"The second's for my neighbor." She jerked her thumb to the wall. "I like to keep him fed."

"Ah." I nodded, then took one of the chairs.

"So you did some explorin' today?"

"I did. This is a beautiful town." I relaxed deeper into the seat. "Have you lived here long?"

"Going on thirty-five years. Me and Sally moved here together in our twenties."

Meggie took my question and ran with it, recounting story after story about life in Summers. I hardly spoke a word, happy to listen to her tales with a smile on my face.

I hated small talk, mostly because it felt forced. When

61

I'd worked for Thomas, it had been. But this felt different, like things had this morning on my walk. Maybe it was the way her hands flew in the air as she spoke. Maybe because she didn't expect me to utter a word. But this small talk felt more like friendship.

She was in the middle of a story about how she and Sally had sunk a boat in the middle of a nearby lake when her eyes lit up and the door opened.

A teenage boy strode inside with two plastic sacks in his grip. "Hi, Miss Meggie."

"Yes, yes. Set 'em down and give me a squeeze." Meggie was off her stool, rounding the counter. She pulled the boy in for a hug, then looked him up and down. "Wyatt, you've grown an inch in a week."

The boy shrugged. "I've been hungry lately."

He was tall, standing at least six inches above Meggie's head. She was about my height, at five five, so I was guessing this kid was close to six feet tall and still growing. He was long and lean but would likely fill out that broad frame.

In a way, he reminded me of Karson at that age. He'd grown fast and long too, so much so that the Cadillac had gotten too small for him to sleep inside. He'd traded the backseat for the outdoors during the warmer months. On the few chilly nights of California winter, he would cram himself in by my side, bitching about how his legs didn't fit.

I smiled, thinking of how I'd curl into his side and fall asleep laughing.

"How's football practice going?" Meggie asked.

Wyatt shrugged again. "Hot."

"Only gonna get hotter." She pinched his cheek—he let her without a wince or fuss—then she dove into the bags he'd brought along. "Say hi to Miss Londyn."

The boy turned and gave me a nod. "Ma'am."

Oof. These West Virginians and their ma'ams.

I stood from my chair and fished out a five-dollar bill from my pocket. I hadn't carried my Louis Vuitton purse anywhere in Summers because it was snobby. I was already planning to donate it somewhere. Besides that, what the hell did I have to cart around? All I needed was some cash and the motel key on the little plastic key chain that read *Room 5.*

"Thanks for the delivery." I held out the money for Wyatt.

His eyes widened. "Oh, that's okay."

"I tipped him," Meggie said.

"Consider it a bonus." I pushed the money into his hand.

I'd survived once on tips. My hourly wage had been shit at the pizza place where I'd worked as a kid. My tips meant I got a new pair of shoes once a year and that I could afford the necessities like toothpaste and tampons.

Since I'd been able to afford it, my tips had become overly generous.

This boy didn't seem to be hurting for money. His Nikes were new and his jeans hadn't come from Goodwill —I could recognize secondhand clothes from a mile away. Wyatt probably didn't need the extra five like I had at his age, but he seemed like the type who'd appreciate it.

He stared at the bill in his hand, then carefully tucked it into his pocket. "Thank you."

"You're welcome."

Wyatt turned and walked to the door, giving Meggie and me another wave and shy grin as he left.

"That boy." She shook her head.

That boy, what? I waited for her to explain, but she only pulled out white Styrofoam containers from the plastic sacks.

"Now I know you might want to disappear into that room of yours." She clicked her tongue. "But if I could make a suggestion?"

"Sure." I collected my meal and a plastic fork.

"There's a nice place to sit behind the motel. It's a rock, so if you're not into nature, then forget it. But it over-looks the lake and you'll get a nice view of the sunset."

"I'm good with nature. Thank you."

"No problem. Technically, it's my neighbor's rock. But since I'm buyin' his dinner, I doubt he'll mind if you borrow it for a night. Now out you go before that curry gets cold."

"Thanks again, Meggie."

She winked, then followed me out the door. As we

rounded the corner of the building, she pointed to the rock past a cluster of trees. "See you tomorrow."

I waved goodbye as she strode across the lawn to her neighbor's house. It was a two-story white home, not new but well maintained. It wasn't fancy, but it was nice. Really nice. Especially with the wide porch that stretched along its front with delicate spindles along the rail. Meggie didn't bother knocking as she marched up to the front door and let herself inside.

What a character. I laughed, turning my attention to the lake.

The rock was easy to spot once I got closer, and Meggie hadn't lied. It was enormous and nearly as long as a picnic table.

It stood about a foot off the ground and I stepped up, settling into the flat surface with my meal on my lap. I was no stranger to eating food perched on my legs. The curry spice and fresh jasmine rice filled my nose as I opened the container.

"Oh my God," I moaned with that first bite. Meggie hadn't lied. This was good curry.

I heaped another bite on my fork, brought it to my mouth, then proceeded to fling the food into the air as a voice came from behind me.

"I see Meggie gave away my favorite dinner table."

A grain of rice lodged in my windpipe. I coughed, choking and my eyes watering, as Brooks rushed over.

"Shit." He slapped me on the back, then rubbed up and down my spine.

I coughed again, managing to dislodge the rice and swallow. My eyes were blurry and my heart was racing when I finally managed to suck in a deep breath.

"Sorry. Thought you heard me walk up."

"No." I put a hand to my chest, taking in more air. "It's okay."

His hand stilled on my spine. "Good?"

"I'm okay." Convenient that Meggie hadn't mentioned Brooks was her neighbor.

I closed the lid on my dinner, setting it aside to stand, but Brooks waved me down. "Stay."

"Oh, no. I can eat in my room."

"This is a big rock. Mind if we share it?" he asked.

"Uh, no."

"Good." He grinned, creating a flutter in my chest. Who grinned like that? Only one corner of his mouth turned up, and *wow* but it was sexy.

Brooks settled on the rock about a foot away, stretching his long legs toward the water. Then I saw why I hadn't heard him approach. He was in bare feet.

Just as sexy as that grin.

He opened his dinner container, closing his eyes as he drew in the smell. When he opened his eyes, he gazed out over the rippled water. "That sure is a good view."

His blue eyes caught the fading sunlight.

Yes, it sure is.

CHAPTER FIVE

BROOKS

Meggie didn't know how *not* to meddle.

I should have known she was up to something when she barged into my house, shoved a takeout container in my hands and proceeded to put away all of the fixings for a ham sandwich I'd just pulled out of the fridge.

Meggie had practically chased me out the back door, telling me to take a night off.

I hadn't argued because I was beat and I knew from the container it was my favorite curry. I'd planned to go back to the garage and catch up on paperwork in the office, but a delicious meal and an evening by the lake had sounded much more appetizing.

Toss Londyn McCormack into the mix and I couldn't help but smile.

She'd been nervous at the garage earlier. I'd never seen

anyone walk that fast in flip-flops. Clearly, she'd stopped in to check on progress. I got it. There were plenty of mechanics in this world who took twice as long as they promised and charged twice as much. Many might see a beautiful woman and think they could take advantage.

That wasn't how I operated, but I didn't blame her for being wary.

"I took your car to the body shop today," I said. "I promise I'm hurrying it along. I know you want to get on the road."

"Oh, I, uh . . . sorry." She gave me an exaggerated frown. "That's not why I came. I don't mean to hover, really. I was just passing by, realized I was hovering and felt bad for interrupting you."

"No interruption at all." She could interrupt me any hour any day of the week. Her face coming through my door had been the best part of my day. Until now.

It was a gorgeous night. The breeze had picked up, softening the heat and adding coolness as the air blew across the water.

"So, Londyn"—I stabbed a piece of chicken—"tell me about yourself."

"You go first."

"But I asked the question." I chuckled. "How about this? Whatever question is asked, we both have to answer. You can ask first."

"I like that. All right." She nodded and turned her gaze out to the water.

I expected something easy. Where was I from. How long had I worked at the garage. Coming up with a personal question didn't seem all that hard, but as the seconds passed into minutes and she remained quiet, I realized why this was hard.

Shit. The reason she wasn't asking wasn't because of *my* answer.

It was because of the one she'd have to give.

"Listen, we don't have to do this. I didn't mean to pry. I'll mind my own business."

"It's not that." She blushed. "I was trying to think of an interesting question, but for the life of me, all I can think of are the boring ones. The pressure got to me."

I chuckled. "Then I'll go first. Where are you from?"

"California is the short answer."

"And the long one?"

Londyn had just taken a bite. She held up her hand as she chewed and my gaze stayed fixed on her profile. It had been a long time since I'd studied a woman's profile, and no surprise, Londyn was beautiful from any angle.

Her nose turned up at the end, just slightly. Was it strange to think someone had a beautiful forehead? Hers had an elegant curve, not too big or flat. Since I'd seen her earlier at the garage, she'd tied up her long blond hair. It was fluffed at the crown, bunched from the ponytail that draped down the center of her shoulders.

She was probably seven or eight inches shorter than my six three. She was thin, but there was strength in her body too, especially those toned legs. Damn, she had legs that didn't quit. Second to her eyes, they were my favorite feature.

She swallowed, using her napkin to wipe her soft, supple lips. "Have you heard of Temecula?"

"No."

"It's about ninety minutes southeast of LA. Great weather, which is a good thing, considering where I lived. When I was sixteen, I ran away from home."

My jaw dropped. "Sixteen?"

"Sixteen," she repeated.

"May I ask why?"

"My parents were more interested in drugs than their daughter." She sighed. "I didn't think anything of it when I was little. Isn't that crazy? I was just a kid and thought everyone's parents were stoned twenty-four seven."

That wasn't crazy but it was sad. A runaway? She didn't seem hard enough to have lived on the streets. She seemed too refined and delicate.

"I learned soon enough it wasn't normal. I learned how to take care of myself. And when things got really bad, I decided it wasn't worth staying."

At sixteen. It was unfathomable. "Where'd you go?"

"I stayed in Temecula, actually. I didn't really have a plan when I left home. I was mad and a teenager and just . . . left. Rational thought didn't really enter the mix at that point."

Yeah. Because she'd been *sixteen*. "I can understand that."

"So I left with a backpack full of clothes and some cash I'd been stealing from my parents. I was going to walk to LA."

"What made you stay?"

"I met a friend. She's my best friend to this day and was living with two other kids in a junkyard outside of town at the time."

"A junkyard?"

Londyn nodded. "Yes. That junkyard became my home for two years. Eventually, six of us lived there. That Cadillac? That's where I lived. I slept in the backseat."

All I could do was blink with my mouth hanging open.

No wonder she hovered over that car.

"Did your parents ever . . ."

"No, they never found me. I don't know if they even looked. As far as I know, they didn't report me missing or contact the police. They just let me go."

My jaw clicked shut and a rage of temper ran through my blood. *Pieces of shit.*

"Don't get angry on me there," Londyn teased, bumping my elbow with her own. "We weren't completely without adult supervision. There was a man who ran the junkyard and watched out for us. It was his property, and Lou let us live there. He let us use the bathroom and shower in his shop. If we got sick, he'd get us medicine."

I blinked at her. "He didn't report it?"

"He knew that if the cops came, we'd be gone. And we were all better off in a junkyard than going back to the hells where we'd come from. He didn't kick us out and that was more than any adult in my life had done for me before."

"Foster care?"

She huffed. "I wasn't going into foster care and no one was going to make me."

"So you lived in a car for two years."

"I did." A small smile toyed on her lips.

She spoke of that place like she'd lived a normal, happy and blessed childhood in a *junkyard*. At sixteen. It wasn't magical, but you'd think it was, looking at her face.

I shook my head. "I-I don't even know what to say."

"I know it seems crazy. But you have to understand, for the first time in my life, I had people who cared about me. The six of us kids and Lou, we were a family. We looked out for one another. We made sure we all had food to eat and clothes to wear."

"What did you do for money? What about school?"

"School was forgotten. But we all worked. We put the junkyard as our address. We used each other's names as our parents' names. I waitressed at a pizza place."

Waitressing was a typical job for a teenager. What had her bosses thought? Had her customers known she'd leave work to go home to a car? "I can't wrap my head around this life."

She laughed, the musical sound drifting out over the

water. "Think of it like camping. We were a bunch of kids who camped every night of the week."

"What did you eat?"

"Easy stuff. Peanut butter and jelly sandwiches. Fast food if we had the money. Bananas. Canned green beans. I brought a lot of pizza back for us to share."

"Hmm." My mind whirled. What would that have been like? At sixteen, I'd been worried about girls and my truck. Would I have survived a runaway life at that age? Definitely not.

Londyn was one tough woman. Tougher than I ever would have guessed. She didn't have manicured nails but she took care with her appearance. Her hair was styled. She had on makeup and though her clothes were casual, they weren't cheap.

And she'd spent two years as a teenager living in a car.

"It's your turn to answer the question."

I scoffed. "Hell, I can't compete with that."

She laughed again, covering her lips with a hand to hide the food she'd just put in her mouth.

I grinned and took a bite, then set my fork aside. "I grew up here in Summers. Born and raised. My parents live here. My grandparents on both sides do too."

"You're lucky."

"Yes, ma'am."

As a kid, I'd known I had it good. But all kids took things for granted. I hadn't appreciated the necessities in my life like clean blankets, healthy food and nice clothes. Compared to her life, I'd lived like a king.

But that wasn't what she was talking about, was it? She didn't feel like she'd missed out on the material things. She knew I was lucky because I had an amazing family.

It made me feel guilty for all the shit I'd put them through.

The good thing was, we'd come out together. My dad was my best friend and my mom was a living saint.

"What happened after California?" I asked. "How'd you get from California to Boston? I'm guessing that Cadillac wasn't in driving condition if it was in a junkyard."

"No." She giggled. "It was a wreck. It came later, after we all went in separate directions. My two friends, Gemma and Katherine, and I took a bus to Montana."

"Why Montana?"

She shrugged. "Why not? We wanted to see what it was like."

"And?" I'd always wanted to visit Montana and camp in Big Sky Country. We had the Appalachians, and they were a world of their own. Once or twice a year, I'd arrange a camping trip to get away and explore. But Montana was a bucket-list trip. "How was it?"

"Beautiful. Raw."

I was jealous at the wonder in her voice. "How long were you there?"

"About four months. Gemma and Katherine stayed

longer. As far as I know, Katherine is still there, but we lost touch."

"And Gemma?"

"She found me in Boston."

"Ah. Did you go straight from Montana to Boston?" I asked.

"Sort of. I made some stops along the way, but nothing lasted longer than a month or two. When I got to Boston, I hadn't planned on staying, but I met someone. We got married and I stayed. Then we got divorced and I left."

Londyn sounded as enthusiastic about her former marriage as I was about mine.

"And now you're on the road."

She nodded. "Yes."

I went back to my meal, eating quietly as she did the same, until another question came to mind. "How'd you get the car from California?"

"I called the junkyard owner and bought it. He didn't remember me at first, but I told him who I was and why I wanted the car. He wanted to give it to me for free but I insisted on paying. Then I had it hauled to Boston and had it restored."

I whistled, visualizing the price tag. It had to be at least a hundred grand. For a woman without much of an education who'd lived her life on the road, how'd she come into that kind of money? Her husband, maybe?

She tossed her fork into the nearly empty container and closed the lid. "That was amazing."

"Not bad for a small town in West Virginia."

"I'm quite impressed with this small town."

My chest swelled with pride at my home.

Londyn and I sat staring out at the water as the bottom of the sun dipped below the horizon. Night wouldn't be far off but I wasn't in a hurry to leave. Londyn didn't seem to be either, so we sat there in comfortable silence, listening to the water lap against the shoreline and the wind rustle the trees.

When was the last time I'd just sat beside a woman? The last time I'd been alone with a woman who wasn't a relative or who wasn't at the shop for an oil change had been over a year ago. A blind date from hell. The woman had talked the entire meal about money. Specifically, my money. She'd wanted to know how much I made at the garage, how much I would inherit from my parents and how much my truck and home were worth.

I'd lost her number before the waitress had delivered our meal.

Sitting with Londyn was different. There were no expectations for conversation. I asked questions not to fill the silence, but because I genuinely wanted to hear her answer. Maybe this was easy because it wasn't a date.

Londyn was leaving Summers in her rearview as soon as her car was fixed.

The lake reflected the yellow, orange and midnight-blue of twilight as tree crickets chirped and lightning bugs sparked.

"You got more than your fair share of the questions tonight," I said. "Sorry."

"That's okay." She tipped her head back to examine the stars above.

I did the same, resting on my elbows. An airplane's light blinked as it flew past.

"Do you ever wish on a star?" she asked.

"Not since I was a kid."

"I used to wish on them every night. The top in the convertible wouldn't raise or lower but the trunk was so wide that I'd lie on it every night and make a wish."

"Any come true?"

"Some." She dropped her back to the rock, lying flat. Her hair splayed over the smooth, brown surface. "I got an education. That was a wish. I didn't want to be the stupidest person in the room anymore."

"I highly doubt that was ever the case." I dropped to my back, lacing my hands behind my head.

"When I was sixteen and working alongside all these other teenagers who were reading *Great Expectations* and Shakespeare, it sure felt like I was stupid. But I worked hard in Boston and got my diploma."

"Did you go to college?"

She shook her head. "No."

"Me neither." I'd planned on college and following in my father's footsteps, but then my life had taken a different path. The good thing was, I'd had some skills to fall back on. "My grandfather started Cohen's Garage. He passed it down to me when he was ready to retire."

"Not your father?"

"No, Dad's a doctor."

"You're a car doctor instead."

"Exactly." I chuckled. "Any other wishes come true?"

"I used to wish for a home—a real home. That one came true in Boston, but then I realized a house and a husband and a paycheck didn't mean I'd be happy."

So she'd left it all behind. Was she still searching for a home? Or had she given that wish up? "Think you'll have a home in California?"

"I don't know. Maybe." She pushed up to sitting. "I might get a job. I might find somewhere new to live for a while. It's not normal, but I think that nomadic lifestyle is more my style. I like the freedom. I didn't realize it until I left Boston, but I was trapped there. I was in a cage."

I sat up too. "So it's you and your car exploring the country." She'd take her home wherever she went.

"Well, the car is going to a friend. But I'll get another. Maybe I'll drive the new one around for the next year. Maybe I'll hop on a plane and explore Europe or Australia or Asia. There's a comfort for me, knowing it's all my decision. I'm not obligated to live my life according to anyone else's plan."

"Huh." I ran a hand through my hair. The idea of travel was exciting, but not having a home to return to seemed lonely to me. But again, we'd come from different worlds. Summers would always be my home.

"Sounds crazy, right?"

"Nah. Just different. I've lived in this town my entire life. I can't imagine living anywhere else." I didn't *want* to live anywhere else, and I was still a free man.

She gave me a sad smile. "I'm glad you have deep roots."

"Me too."

She held my gaze, enchanting me with every passing second. What a life she'd lived. What a story. And now she'd give in to her wanderlust and see the world. What an adventure it would be to go along for the ride.

Her eyes glowed green in the fading light. When we'd sat up, we'd shifted closer together. All I had to do was lean over and I could take her lips in a kiss. I'd thought about those soft lips a lot the past day, wondering what she'd taste like. Would she kiss me back? Or would she dump the rest of her curry over my head? Maybe I'd misread the blushes and shy smiles.

Londyn's eyes dropped to my mouth. *Fuck it.* She was leaving and I might as well go for broke. I had just dipped low, brushing my lips against hers, when a car door slammed on the street behind us.

She jumped, breaking us apart.

Damn. The universe was telling me something. This woman, who'd be a memory before the week was out, was not for me.

"Probably better head home. It's getting late." I sighed, collecting my container and stacking hers on top. Then I stood, holding out a hand to help her up.

"Thanks." She brushed off the seat of her shorts and I didn't let myself look at her ass—much.

I stepped off the rock first, my bare feet sinking into the lush grass.

She hopped down behind me. "Thanks for not kicking me off your rock."

"Anytime."

"Good night, Brooks." She waved, then started toward the motel.

I lifted my arm to wave goodbye. I couldn't bring myself to do it.

There was something fresh about her. Maybe it was her outlook on life or her spirit. Maybe it was that she had gone through so much and she hadn't become jaded or cynical. Londyn intrigued me. She stirred my blood.

And damn it, I hadn't had enough time tonight. I wanted more, not just to give that kiss another go, but to talk.

I should let her go.

"Londyn?" I called.

"Yes?" She turned, flashing me those gorgeous green eyes.

"You feel like sharing the rock again tomorrow night?"

She smiled. "Yes."

CHAPTER SIX

LONDYN

"That's a lot of meat. There's no way I can fit this in my mouth."

Brooks cocked an eyebrow. "The words any man wants to hear."

"Get your mind out of the gutter." I rolled my eyes, then hefted the sandwich he'd brought me to my mouth and attempted a bite.

The thing was a foot long and weighed at least a pound—a solid brick of meat and cheese with a sprinkling of shredded lettuce and tomatoes. Oil and vinegar coated it all and a thick, sturdy loaf of bread acted more like a boat than bookends.

"Yum." I hummed as I chewed, my cheeks bulging.

"Good, right?"

"So good." The words came out garbled.

He laughed, then took a bite of his own, groaning as he ate.

As with all other things Brooks Cohen, that groan of his was damn sexy. It was low and deep, more like a hum coming from his heart than a sound formed from his voice box. It was soft too—if I wasn't sitting within a foot of his side, I would have missed out.

Tonight was the third night in a row I'd eaten on the lakeside rock with Brooks. Thai that first time. Last night he'd brought pasta. And tonight, subs. Three delicious meals made more so because of the company.

We ate in silence, like the other nights, neither of us anxious to fill the quiet moments. It was like sharing a meal with an old friend, not a new acquaintance. We'd talk later. The sun had yet to drop over the horizon so there'd be time. Brooks would ask questions and I'd soak up his own answers. Last night, we'd stayed out stargazing and talking about nothing until nearly eleven.

These three meals had been three of the most relaxing I'd had in years. I didn't have a phone buzzing and demanding attention. There was no talk about work, something I realized now had been the constant theme whenever talking with Thomas.

Conversation with Brooks was a discovery. A slow, stirring journey that spanned numerous topics. He'd told me about his parents and growing up in Summers. I'd told him about my life in Boston, skirting around the details of my divorce.

The truth was, I hadn't thought much about Thomas in the past few days. I didn't miss him—hadn't for months. I didn't yearn for the early days of our marriage, when there had been more joy and thrill. Though things had taken a hard turn at the end, a part of me was glad we were over.

Would I have left otherwise? If there hadn't been Secretary and the affair, would I have ever realized how unhappy I'd become?

Money had blinded me. I wasn't in love with Thomas. My job had lost its appeal. That life was devoid of passion.

Passion, I did miss.

Which was probably another reason the last three nights had been so refreshing. Passion and anticipation coated each minute I spent with Brooks like warm chocolate on vanilla bean ice cream. It took every second to the next, delicious level.

He hadn't made a move to kiss me again. Would he try again tonight? My time in Summers was coming to a close. I wasn't sure I'd be able to drive away without at least one kiss to take with me. It would be a memory I'd tuck into my pocket to pull out and replay on the lonely days.

"I picked up your car before I came tonight," Brooks said. "It's all done. Good as new."

"Really? Okay." That was disappointing. Expected, since he'd promised three or four days, but disappointing. As a show of faith, I hadn't asked Brooks about my car. Or maybe I hadn't asked because I was content for the moment.

Brooks swallowed the last bite of his sandwich. How he could eat all that and maintain a flat stomach was borderline unfair. I'd only made it through a third of mine and was stuffed. I wrapped it in the paper and set it aside.

"You'll be back on the road tomorrow."

Did I hear a hint of disappointment in his voice? Or was I projecting my own? "That's fantastic."

Liar. Maybe I could stay longer? I didn't have a schedule. This trip was all about me and going at my own pace. Tempting, but every night spent on this rock with Brooks would only make me hold out for the next.

I *could* stay, but I wouldn't. The time had come to move along to the next stop on this adventure. Once Karson had the Cadillac and I'd satisfied my curiosity about his life, I would be free to wander and go at my own pace.

"Brooks?" A woman's voice carried across the yard behind us. We both twisted, looking past a tree trunk.

"Damn it," Brooks grumbled, pushing up to his feet. "Be back."

"Okay."

He jogged across the yard, once again in bare feet, and met the woman as she came down from his porch. She wore black sunglasses that hid most of her face. Her brown hair was pulled up into a purposefully messy knot on the top of her head. The summer dress she wore wrapped around her body, tying tight underneath her generous breasts.

She was beautiful, and clearly upset with my dinner companion. She planted her hands on her waist and screwed up her mouth in a tight line as Brooks spoke. When it was her turn to talk, she cast a scowl my way.

Shit. She'd caught me staring. Should I hide? Who was she?

I hadn't asked if Brooks had a girlfriend. Considering we sat outside his house, I was certain he wasn't married. I'd made the assumption that he was the kind of man who wouldn't be sharing dinner with a woman if he were otherwise entangled.

Maybe that was stupid on my part. My husband had just cheated on me. But, call it a gut feeling, Brooks didn't seem to be the straying kind.

He was a man who bought a woman a cell phone because he didn't like the idea of her on the road without the ability to call for help. He was a gentleman in the truest sense of the word, putting me first in everything from opening a door to taking the first bite of a meal.

Not wanting to stare as he spoke to the woman, I turned my attention to the lake. I sipped the bottle of water he'd brought me as a speedboat raced through the calm water in the distance. It traveled fast, a white fleck on the water by the time Brooks came back.

"Sorry about that." He hopped up on the rock.

"That's okay. Do you need to go?" An engine started

in the distance and I glanced over my shoulder as the woman reversed a Honda out of his driveway.

"No. That was my ex-wife, Moira."

"Ah." Of course she'd be beautiful. I bet she'd made a beautiful bride in a white gown, walking to a handsome Brooks in a tux, standing at an altar. My mental picture was tinged with green.

When was the last time I'd gotten jealous? Had I been jealous of Secretary? Hurt, yes. Betrayed, absolutely. But jealous? Not really.

Had his house been Moira's home? Had she shared this rock too?

"Do you ever swim in the lake?" I blurted.

It was an odd question, given the moment, but I didn't want to talk to Brooks about his ex-wife. I sensed he didn't either. Especially on our last night.

"Sometimes." Brooks went along with my change of subject. "When it's hot."

"I only learned to swim five years ago." My parents hadn't put me in swim lessons, and I'd been busy working my summers away instead of spending them at the community pool. On my honeymoon, I'd stayed safely in a lounge chair.

It wasn't until Thomas had insisted on scuba diving on a trip to the Caribbean that I'd had to admit I didn't know how to swim. He'd insisted on lessons.

"I was supposed to take private lessons, but when I got to the pool, there had been a mix-up and they'd put me in the kids' class. They offered to switch things around, but I stayed. The kids didn't care that a grown woman couldn't swim. I wasn't quite as pathetic."

"There's a lot of folks who live around here, around this lake, and don't swim." Brooks nudged my shoulder with his. "It's not pathetic."

I smiled. "Thanks."

The inability to swim hadn't been important until Thomas had pointed out I was lacking. He seemed to find more flaws with me than I did myself. Each time he realized I'd missed something in my youth that set me apart from other cultured adults, he remedied it immediately.

Londyn hasn't ridden a horse? He bought me a horse and had it stabled with a riding instructor.

Londyn can't tell the difference between merlot and cabernet? He hired a sommelier to join us for dinner three nights a week.

Londyn doesn't like the opera? He bought season tickets because I hadn't been enough to appreciate it.

I hated the fucking opera. Red wine, no matter the grape, tasted like red wine. And horses scared the piss out of me.

Yep. I didn't miss him at all.

A bird chirped loudly from above, causing me to turn. It was perched in a tree next to Brooks's back deck. "I like your house."

"Thanks." He turned, taking in the back of his house too. "I bought it after the divorce."

That answered my earlier question about Moira. "It's nice. Very quaint."

The Victorian style was complete with tall roof peaks and curled gables in their apex. On the rear side of the home, overlooking the backyard, two dormer windows emerged from the chocolate roof. The rest of the home was white. The only thing that differentiated the various sides and sections of the exterior walls was the texture. Some of the siding was horizontal boards, other parts overlapping scallops.

"I love all the windows." The abundance of paned glass meant that most rooms were probably flooded with daylight.

"Same. That's what sold me on the place. In the summer I don't have to set an alarm. I wake up with the sun."

"I haven't set an alarm since Boston. I used to wake up at four every morning. I'd go to the gym and come home to get ready for work. In the winter, I'd be up for hours before the sunrise. Maybe I'll get up with the sun from now on too."

"Some days the alarm is unavoidable," he said. "There are days when I've got a lot happening in the shop. I've never quite mastered staying ahead on office work. It was really bad in the beginning when I took over for Grand-dad. I had a hell of a time keeping up. Figured it out eventually though. Tony helps keep me from drowning."

"Do you like your job?"

"Yes." His one-word answer held so much truth. Brooks *loved* his job, without a doubt. "What did you do in Boston?"

"I worked for my husband's company as his assistant." I turned to the lake again.

"Did you like it?"

"Yes, I did, actually. It was the first job where I was challenged. And Thomas was great about letting me pick and choose what I wanted to work on. I started out with the easy stuff. Phones and scheduling meetings into his calendar. But it grew."

I liked to think he'd suffered some at work after I'd quit. That was my ego talking, but no one wanted to admit they were easily replaceable.

"I've thought about getting an office manager," Brooks said. "Someone who can do the bookkeeping and order parts and keep the papers from stacking up on my desk. I sure wouldn't miss it. I'd much rather work on cars. Use my hands."

He had great hands. His fingers were long and calloused at the tips. His palms were wide and soft in the center. I was envious of my own damn car. The Cadillac had felt those hands skim across her surface.

"I wasn't sure exactly when you'd have the car done. You said a few days, but I didn't think you'd have it ready so soon."

"No faith in me?" He feigned a wince. "I'm hurt."

"You've exceeded all my expectations."

"My pleasure." His deep, soothing drawl was so comforting, it gave me the courage to ask the question on my mind.

"When I booked my room, I had it through tomorrow. I don't want to cancel on Meggie with such short notice. If I stayed one more night, would you go to dinner with me?"

I held my breath. It was the first time in my life I'd asked a man on a date. But he'd say yes. Right? He was enjoying these dinners as much as I was, wasn't he? Otherwise, why would he have invited me here each night?

"I, uh . . ." Brooks ran a hand through his hair. "I can't. Sorry."

My heart plummeted. *Ouch.* "That's okay."

A tense silence stretched between us. Brooks didn't offer any explanation as to why he couldn't meet me tomorrow. I sat perfectly still, unsure what to say. Maybe he had to work late. Maybe he didn't like eating at restaurants. Maybe he had a date. If that was the reason, I didn't want to know.

Without dinner tomorrow, this was the last time I'd spend with Brooks. I'd see him at the shop tomorrow morning when I collected my car, but it would be a brief farewell before I left Summers and Brooks Cohen behind for good.

My stomach clenched. It had to be the sandwich, not the idea of leaving. I'd simply eaten too much.

Time to go. The urge to leave hit hard, shoving me to my feet. Staying until dark wasn't going to happen tonight.

I didn't have a wish to make. "I'd better get going. I need to pack."

"Londyn." Brooks stood, blocking the way off the rock. "Don't. Not yet."

"I think it's for the best." I met his blue gaze and my resolve to walk away broke. There was so much apology in those eyes. So much longing.

"I—" Without finishing, he closed his mouth and shifted, making room for me to walk past.

We both knew it was better to end this before things got complicated.

It wasn't like I didn't have some memories to take along. I'd look back on my time in Summers and remember this handsome man who'd been my dinner date three nights in a row. I'd remember this rock and how I preferred it to any table. I'd remember that almost kiss.

"Thank you," I said as he joined me on the grass. "It was lovely to know you, Brooks."

"Likewise, Londyn." He held out his hand and I slipped mine into his grip.

Neither of us let go.

He tightened his hold, pulling me closer. His gaze dropped to my lips and my breath hitched. Was he going to kiss me after all? It would certainly ease the sting of rejection. He leaned closer. My eyes drifted closed.

A whisper of a breath floated across my cheek as his mouth came down and he planted a kiss.

On. My. Cheek.

Disappointment flamed it red. My pride turned black and blue and I pulled my hand free of his grasp. "Good night, Brooks."

He took a step back. "Night, Londyn."

Then I spun around and marched for my motel room.

Time to get the hell out of Summers, West Virginia.

And far away from Brooks Cohen.

———

CLANK.

I jumped at the noise as it echoed from the garage. I stalled outside the door, not sure if I should get any closer. Was that normal garage noise? Because it sounded really loud. When nothing followed, I took another step.

Clank. Thud. Clank.

I jumped again, gasping at the bangs and clashes that came in a steady stream.

"Goddamn it!" Brooks roared.

Then came another crash. This one sounded like metal hitting metal, followed by the clink and clatter of tools hitting the concrete floor.

"Fuck!"

Uh . . . What the hell was going on? Was he hurt? I stepped forward, not sure what to expect, and peered around the door.

Brooks was pacing beside my car, his fists clenched in fury and his chest heaving.

I followed his gaze.

"What happened to my car?" I shrieked, stepping inside.

Long scratches ran up the length of the red paint. They were thin and narrow, angry as they cut through the smooth surface. It wasn't as bad as when I'd skidded into the guardrail, but it wasn't good either. The trunk was covered in yellow. The paint dripped to the floor, puddling next to a tire.

My hands dove into my hair. "Oh my God."

"Londyn, I can explain." Brooks held out a hand.

"Yes. Please." I nodded, unable to look away from the wreckage.

"Someone broke in last night and vandalized the place."

I tore my eyes away from the Cadillac and took in the rest of the garage. The same yellow paint on my car had been splashed on one of the cinderblock walls. Tools were scattered across the floor. Tires that had been stacked against the far wall were strewn around. There was another car in the opposite bay but it looked unharmed.

"Who would do this?"

Brooks sighed, planting his fists on his hips. "I don't know."

"Take a guess." This was a small town. He had to have some idea who would do this to me. And the narrowed look on his face said he definitely had an idea.

"Moira."

His ex-wife? "Why?" Was this because she'd seen us sitting on that rock last night? "I'm no one. I'm leaving. Or I was until this."

His lips pursed into a thin line. "She gets jealous. She knows I've got a thing for you."

"Oh." My anger flatlined. "You do?"

"Think that's pretty obvious, don't you?"

"But you didn't kiss me last night." He'd rejected my date.

"No, I didn't." He walked to the Cadillac, leaning against the scratched side panel. I couldn't see the driver's side, but I was guessing it hadn't fared well either. "That was my mistake, and I regretted it all night long."

I'd sulked for hours as I'd slowly packed up my suitcases last night, wishing things had ended differently. I guess I'd get that wish because there'd be no goodbye today.

"What about my car?"

"I'll wash off the paint, but it'll have to go back to the body shop for the scratches."

I stepped closer, running my finger over a scratch. "Is that from a key?"

"Yeah," he muttered.

"You don't sound surprised."

"No." He blew out a deep breath. "I'm sorry. I'll pay to have it fixed, but it will take a while."

"Ironic, isn't it? If your ex is jealous, she should have just left me alone. I would have been gone."

Brooks pushed off the car and strode my way. "I'm so sorry, Londyn."

"It's not your fault."

"You'd be on your way if I had stayed away from you."

Even if I could get in my car right now, I wasn't sure that was what I wanted. "Make it up to me?"

"Absolutely. How?"

"Dinner tonight."

His chin fell. "I can't tonight."

Damn. Twice? "You keep shooting me down and it's killing my ego," I muttered.

"I can't do dinner. But how about that kiss?"

My eyes whipped up as he crossed the distance between us, his hands leading the way. They came to my face, cupping my cheeks and angling my head to the side. He inched closer until his boots touched my shoes. "Well?"

I nodded.

Brooks swept down and captured my mouth, stealing all the breath from my lungs. I went up on my tiptoes as his tongue swept across my bottom lip, the gentleman seeking permission. I opened for him, letting him dive in deep.

His hands stayed on my face, pulling me to him as he let one of those low groans loose, down my throat. It sent a rush to my core. His taste exploded on my tongue, the lingering bitterness of coffee mixed with his own sweetness. His tongue dueled with mine as those soft lips pressed hard.

I would have pegged Brooks as the type to go for soft and sweet at first, but there was nothing gentle or demure about this kiss. He took what he wanted, demanding more. It was hot and I'd feel his fingertips on my face for the rest of the day.

Other than our mouths, it was the only place we touched.

I didn't dare bring my hands to his chest. I didn't dare risk wrapping my arms around his waist or sidling my hips toward his. Brooks was in charge and he was doing a damn fine job without my help.

The kiss ended too quickly. He pulled away, letting me go as he wiped his mouth, leaving a smug smirk in place.

"Th-thanks." I was off-balance. "I feel better about my car."

He chuckled. "Same."

"So, I'll, uh . . . go." I took a step backward, pointing to the exit. If I didn't get out of here, there was a good chance I'd crawl my way up his body and we'd do a lot more than kiss. I spun around as a smile spread across my face.

"Londyn?" he called.

"Yeah?"

"Sorry about the car."

I glanced over my shoulder. "I'm not."

CHAPTER SEVEN

BROOKS

I raised my fist and pounded on my ex-wife's door. We'd been divorced for a decade but it still felt strange to knock after living here for years.

Moira's heels clicked across the wood floor I'd installed the year before moving out. She had a smile on her face when she answered the door—it dropped when she spotted me.

"Hi." She was wearing a simple black dress, as she did most summer days when she worked. In the winter, she'd add a cardigan. Moira was a receptionist at a dentist's office, and to most, she looked poised and professional. But I knew a viper lurked underneath the surface.

Moira was incredible when she wanted to be. When she didn't, her claws left a nasty mark.

"Why'd you do it?" I didn't bother with a greeting. We were beyond playing nice.

She was lucky I'd waited until after five to come to her house instead of marching down to Dr. Kurt's office and having this out with her at work.

"Do what?" She crossed her arms over her chest.

"Don't play dumb." I frowned. "That's my place of business."

"What are you talking about?"

"The last time you came in and messed up the place, you set me back a week. But you crossed the line here. You fucked with a customer's car."

"Are you drunk?" She leaned forward. "I haven't been to the garage in months."

It was always the same with her. Lie, lie, lie. Even when she knew she was caught, she never admitted defeat.

"Whatever. Stay the fuck away from my garage. The next time, I'm calling the cops."

"I didn't do anything, Brooks."

"Sure." *Heard that before too.* I spun on my boot and marched down the sidewalk.

"Brooks," she snapped.

I didn't answer.

"Brooks!"

I strode to my pickup.

"Fuck you." Now the fangs were out. Was it really a wonder we hadn't made it? I was almost to my pickup when she yelled, "Wait. Please."

I sighed, pausing on the sidewalk. "Yeah?"

"Are you coming tomorrow?"

I scoffed. "No."

"You promised."

"I said I'd think about it. I have, and I'm not coming."

"Grr," she snarled, stepping inside the house and slamming the door. It echoed down the block.

Typical. That wasn't the first time she'd slammed that door on me. I'd had enough of her bullshit to last a lifetime.

Moira had come over last night and asked me over for dinner. Her parents were coming to town tomorrow and had hoped to see me. It was something we'd done over the years, even after the divorce. I wasn't a fan of my ex but her parents were good people.

I'd have to catch them the next time. Tomorrow I'd still be fuming mad at their daughter.

The key marks in the Cadillac had Moira written all over them. A year after our divorce, I'd dated the new kindergarten teacher in town. Things had been going pretty well for about a month, then she'd called me one Sunday morning and told me we were over without explanation.

I'd found out a week later it was because Moira had keyed the hell out of my girlfriend's car.

I hadn't dated for two years after that. But then I'd finally met a nice woman who'd worked with Dad at the hospital. Moira hadn't even given us a month. Six dates in and Moira had slashed her tires. All four of them.

She'd admitted to that one eventually, after the nurse

99

had moved away from Summers. She'd gotten drunk one night and called me in tears, begging for a second chance. When I'd assured her it would never fucking happen, she'd gotten nasty and vowed no woman would ever hang around for long.

Years later, I guess she still meant it.

Moira's antics had cost me stress and money I could have used for much better things. I'd paid to have the key marks fixed and the tires replaced. But I hadn't bothered to date since. No woman I'd met had seemed worth the drama.

Until Londyn.

Even after I'd admitted it was likely my ex-wife who'd trashed her car, Londyn hadn't run away screaming. She'd asked me out. Then she'd let me kiss the hell out of her.

I grinned over the steering wheel. Londyn McCormack was one of a kind.

Traffic was light, per usual, as I drove across Summers toward my parents' place. We had a standing dinner every Monday night—had for sixteen years. Tonight was one of the few times I'd contemplated skipping.

I looked forward to Mom's cooking and shooting the breeze with Dad over a glass of scotch. But I had a limited number of nights with Londyn. More now than there had been this morning.

Moira's plan had backfired. Maybe she'd meant to chase Londyn out of town, but she didn't understand Londyn's attachment to that car. Most wouldn't unless they knew her story. That Cadillac was woven into her life. It was her childhood home brimming with fond memories.

She wouldn't leave Summers until it was in pristine condition, which gave me time. It might even take a week.

I'd called Mack at the body shop and explained the situation to him. After a string of curses, he'd agreed to fit it into their schedule again as well as cut me a break. He knew what Moira was like. But he didn't have the flexibility he'd had last week. I'd driven the Cadillac over and he'd promised to hurry.

We'd left it at that. My guess? Londyn would be on her way in a week.

One more week. Maybe she'd let me kiss her again.

Five minutes away from Mom and Dad's place, my phone buzzed with a text. They lived on fifty acres about ten miles out of town.

Mom: I didn't feel like cooking today. How about a pizza?

Pizza? I wasn't missing one of the few nights I'd have with Londyn for pizza. I pulled up Mom's number and sent the call through.

"I just texted you," she answered.

"I saw that. How mad would you be if I didn't make it for pizza?" My foot hovered over the brake.

"Hmm." A frown invaded her voice. "You never miss Monday dinner."

"Yeah, I know." I put my foot back on the gas. I *never*

missed Monday dinner. The guilt was too much to live with.

"Is this about the garage?" Mom asked. "I heard what happened. I'm so sorry."

No shock Mom had heard. Tony had a big mouth. He'd come into the shop today, whistled and gotten right to work putting the place back to sorts. The two of us had had it all fixed before noon. While I'd spent my lunch hour catching up on everything I hadn't done over the morning, he'd disappeared.

Now I knew where he'd gone—to gossip with Sally.

"It's fine. No major damage." Except Londyn's car.

"Do you know who might have done it?"

Oh yeah, I knew. But Mom didn't need to know it was Moira. "Probably kids."

As far as the world was concerned, Moira and I had survived an amicable divorce. We were friendly in public. We supported one another though we lived separate lives. We smiled and played nice.

For Wyatt.

I'd been seventeen years old when my son was born. Moira and I had been high school sweethearts. Two stupid kids who thought they were invincible and that condoms were reasonable, not required.

We'd done our best as teenage parents. I hadn't spent my senior year in high school submitting college applications and making campus visits. I'd spent my free time after class at the garage working because it was the key to my son's survival.

Moira had lived with her parents until Wyatt was born, then she'd moved into my parents' place. After graduation, we'd married but lived with Mom and Dad until Wyatt was two.

The reason I didn't miss a Monday dinner was because Mom and Dad had helped us raise Wyatt those first two years. Mom had taught Moira how to feed him and rock him to sleep. She had taught me how to change a diaper and make a bottle for a midnight feeding. Dad had been Wyatt's doctor from the moment he screamed his first breath.

When my parents had needed a break, Moira's had stepped in to help.

Mom didn't ask me for much. Monday dinners weren't mandatory but I knew she looked forward to them. It was her special evening to spend with her husband, son and grandson.

Wyatt had been with Moira this past week. The great thing about us living in the same town, ten minutes from one another, was he had two rooms. He stayed with her for a week to ten days, then he'd come and stay with me for the same.

Now that he was a teenager and had his own vehicle, we didn't dictate custody schedules. Plus he was a good kid, making sure he spent time with us both.

This stretch at Moira's was going on seven days, and I missed him. We texted. I called him every day. But it was strange not to see him every night. With his summer football practice schedule and the job he'd taken running takeout around town, he was busy. It was the reason I ordered takeout most nights when he wasn't at my place. He was forced to come see me.

That, and no matter where he was staying, he came to Monday dinner.

As much as I wanted to see Londyn tonight, I needed my son more.

"Want me to go pick up pizza?" I asked Mom.

"You're coming?"

"I just pulled into the driveway."

She hung up on me and had the screen door open before I'd even shut off my truck. As long as it was light out and the temperature was above fifty degrees, Mom kept her front door open with only the screen to block the bugs.

She shooed me away as I walked to the door. "You can go."

"I'll stay." I met her by the door, bending to kiss her cheek.

"Go. Besides, your son just texted me. Apparently, no one but me and your father want pizza tonight."

My forehead furrowed, taking my phone from my pocket. "Wyatt didn't text—never mind."

Wyatt: I got offered an extra shift tonight. Can I take it?

He was desperately trying to save money for college.

Me: Sure.

Wyatt: Coming home tonight. Be there about ten.

Me: Drive safe.

"He's working," I told Mom, tucking my phone away again. But I'd get to see him tonight.

"He's a hard worker, that boy. Like his daddy." She nudged my elbow. "Go. Do what you need to do. I'll cook something fancy next Monday to make up for this week."

"Are you sure?"

She smiled. "I'm sure."

"Thanks, Mom." I kissed her cheek once more, then turned and jogged to my truck. I waved goodbye as I pulled away, then headed toward town, calling the motel as I drove.

"Hi, Meggie. Say, I need a favor."

———

"IS THIS SEAT TAKEN?"

Londyn's head whipped my way. "What are you doing here? I thought you were busy."

"Change of plan." I pulled out the stool by her side, leaning my elbows on the counter.

The diner was packed. Every booth was taken and all the tables in the middle of the room occupied. Besides the stool I'd just claimed, only two others were empty.

The waitress brought over a menu, but I waved it away.

"You're not eating?" Londyn asked.

"I am, but I don't need a menu. I've ordered the same thing in this diner for the past fifteen years. A cheeseburger with extra pickles and no onion. Fries. A chocolate shake. This waitress is new to town, otherwise she wouldn't have bothered with the menu."

Londyn blinked.

"What? I'm hungry." I shrugged. "It was a busy day."

"Uh-huh," she muttered. "What are you doing here?"

I spun in my stool, giving her my full attention as I leaned in close. The vanilla scent of her hair caught my notice, the sweetness beating out even the grease wafting from the kitchen. The shuffle of forks and knives, the drone of conversation in the background, all disappeared.

Our noses were practically touching. No one in the room would mistake my intention, Londyn included. "I'm here for you, honey."

A smile tugged at the corner of her luscious mouth.

The kiss in the garage had replayed in my mind on a loop today. The memory of her soft lips and the slide of her tongue had distracted me more than once as I'd worked. I didn't care that we were in a restaurant full of people. I needed another taste.

"Here you go, ma'am." The waitress broke the moment, bringing back the noise, as she slid a plate in front of Londyn.

"You ordered pie?" And not just one slice but three. The diner's famous apple—my favorite—the chocolate cream and Wyatt's favorite, cherry.

"I did." She picked up her fork. "I used to go to the grocery store as a kid and buy the pies they had on sale. You know, the day-old ones they sell cheap. When I was living with my parents, I'd hide in my bedroom and eat the whole thing myself. At the junkyard, I'd buy one if I had the money and share. But then diets and exercise became a thing and I didn't eat pie for dinner anymore. Tonight, I said fuck it."

I chuckled. "Good for you."

"When was the last time you had pie for dinner?"

"Can't say I ever have."

Her fork dove into the chocolate cream. She hummed and her eyes drifted closed when the bite passed her lips. She savored it, rolling it around in her mouth. The woman had a talented tongue—lucky pie. She moaned again, torturing me with the subtle sound.

She swallowed, then shot me a smile that was pure sex. "You're missing out."

I snapped my fingers, raising my hand in the air to flag down the waitress. When she came over, I pointed to Londyn's plate. "I'll have that."

Londyn laughed, going in for another bite.

It didn't take the waitress long to serve up my pie. I dug into the apple first. "Damn, that's good. I'll probably give myself a bellyache with this, but I'm not leaving a bite behind."

"Some mistakes are worth the consequences."

"True," I said. "What was the last mistake you made that you didn't regret?"

She tilted up her chin and cast her eyes upward, the way she did whenever she was thinking over one of my questions. When she had her answer, she looked at me with those bright green eyes sparkling. "I wasn't paying attention to the road when I got that flat tire. I was mad at myself at the time. Now, not so much."

"I'm rather fond of that flat tire, myself."

Londyn giggled, taking a stab at the cherry. "Your turn."

A mistake I didn't regret? Easy answer. *Wyatt.*

I opened my mouth to tell her about him but stopped short. He was the most important person in my life. He was my pride and joy. And though I was fond of Londyn, before I shared him with her, I'd share her with him first.

Tonight. I didn't need Moira to make an under-the-breath comment about how I was hooking up with a woman from the motel.

Wyatt had been after me to start dating again, probably because he'd had a string of girlfriends this past year. He was a star on the football and basketball teams and had inherited my tall build. After the games, the girls all flocked his direction.

Thankfully, he had more common sense than I'd had

at his age, and he assured me he hadn't had sex yet. And when he did, he promised to be safe.

I shoved another bite in my mouth to stop myself from bragging about my son. The praise was begging to be set free. Instead, I found a different answer to her question.

"The shop. About three years after I took it over from Granddad, I had a guy ask if he could buy it. I got greedy and asked for twice what he'd offered. He told me to shove it and left town. After that, I regretted it for years. Until one day, I just . . . didn't. I wouldn't give that shop up for anything in the world."

Someday, I'd pass it down to Wyatt if he had any interest. At the moment, I was just glad it was me and not some other lucky bastard who had the only tow truck in town and had been sent to rescue Londyn.

"I'm glad you didn't sell your shop," she said. "We don't know each other well, but I honestly can't imagine you doing anything else."

"Same here." I'd found my dream job at eighteen. Not many could say that.

We ate the rest of our pies, talking about nothing, until both plates were clear and my stomach bulged. I paid the check, shooting Londyn a scowl when she reached for her purse. Then I followed her out of the diner, ignoring the eyes on us as I placed my hand on the small of her back.

"May I give you a ride?" I asked, waving to my truck down the block.

"How'd you know where I was? Wait." She held up her hand. "Let me guess. Meggie."

"You'd be correct." I walked to the truck.

Londyn stayed on the sidewalk. "If I get in with you, what kind of payback can I expect from your ex-wife?"

I grumbled and kicked at a stone on the sidewalk. "I don't know. I don't know what she's thinking."

She wasn't, that was the problem. Moira had likely done her worst already, but I also hadn't had a woman in my life like Londyn. Sure, the others had been nice. I'd enjoyed dating them. But Londyn was different. There was passion and urgency. She was leaving and I was determined to make the most of this while I had the chance.

We were moving at warp speed here—no choice otherwise. That wouldn't escape Moira's notice. Neither would the hole left behind when Londyn left Summers.

"It doesn't matter." She stepped off the curb, meeting me by the door. "I'm not scared of your ex-wife."

Of course she wasn't. I grinned. "Good."

"We have an audience," she whispered.

"Yep," I whispered back. "Why do people think that just because I'm standing outside and they're sitting inside behind a window, we can't see them?"

Londyn giggled. "I can feel them staring."

"I want to kiss you." I inched closer.

Londyn rose up slightly off her heels. "But you probably shouldn't."

"No." Not with half the damn town staring. And not before I had a discussion with Wyatt.

I reached past her and opened the truck's door. Londyn climbed in, letting me shut her in, before I rounded the tailgate for my own side.

I frowned at the people in the diner, still staring, then started up the engine and backed away. Hell, I hadn't kissed her, but just taking her to the motel would probably stir the rumor mill.

"Why do I have a feeling that after tonight, a lot more people will know my name?" she asked.

I chuckled. "Small-town life."

She hummed.

Was that a good hum? Or a bad? She seemed to like this small town, for the time being. But I wasn't going to get my hopes up that Londyn would stay.

"What are we doing tomorrow?" she asked as the motel's sign came into view down the street.

"You assume we'll be doing something together?" I teased.

"Yes."

I shot her a wink. "I like that."

I had ideas for tomorrow night. Wyatt had football practice twice, once in the morning and another late afternoon. Then he'd be rushing off to work until the five restaurants in town that used him and a couple other kids to deliver were closed. My ideas for Londyn involved a repeat of that kiss we'd had in the shop, this time in a place where we could make it last.

"How about we start off with dinner?" That seemed to be working well for us.

"A restaurant or the rock?"

The rock. I wanted time alone with her, not with the town of Summers watching. "Your choice."

She flashed me that sexy smile. "The rock."

CHAPTER EIGHT

LONDYN

"Goddamn, you can kiss," Brooks panted as he hovered above me. His lips were flushed and swollen. His hair was disheveled from where I'd had it between my fingers. Twilight danced around us and the fading light brought out the darker blue striations in his eyes. He'd gone from gorgeous to fucking magnificent.

The most handsome man on earth wasn't a Times Square model or a Hollywood dreamboat. He was a mechanic in West Virginia.

And for the time being, he was mine.

Maybe if I had three more nights like this, I'd have his features memorized for life.

Brooks rolled away, lying flat on his back at my side. Our hands were nearly touching, but not quite.

My chest heaved as my shoulders pressed into the hard rock. I gazed up into the sky, bringing a hand to my lips. Three nights of making out like teenagers and they'd been rubbed raw.

All we'd done was kiss. Brooks always stopped us before we could go too far. So I had chapped lips and an ache in my core that hurt.

This kissing was taking a toll on Brooks too. He shifted uncomfortably, cocking a knee to hide the bulge in his jeans. An impressive bulge at that, especially when it was digging into my hip.

We'd both be going to sleep frustrated tonight. I refused to release some of the tension on my own. If and when Brooks decided to let go of the ironclad grip he had on his control, I wanted this eager desire burning hot under the surface. For once, I was letting the foreplay drive me wild.

With other men, Thomas included, kissing had become a boring preview to a boring feature title. But damn, it was fun with Brooks. I'd forgotten how fun kissing could be on its own.

Something told me that even after we had sex—if we had sex—kissing would always be an event of its own.

Well, for the days I was here.

Lying by his side, it was easy to forget this situation was temporary. Brooks erased the future with his lips. All that mattered was now. Here. My future was on this rock with nature's symphony drowning out reality.

Brooks stretched a finger to touch one of mine. "What are you thinking about?"

"I'm leaving."

"Yeah." He covered my hand with his. "But not yet."

I smiled, turning my head to look at him. His grin was waiting. "No, not yet."

My car was at the body shop and the crew there hadn't even started on it yet. They could take their time. If it was done tomorrow, I doubted I'd leave anyway.

I wasn't done with Summers yet. I wasn't done kissing Brooks.

He raised his left hand, taking a glance at his watch. "I'd better get on home soon."

Brooks had sent me on my way before ten each night. The stars were barely coming alive as I sulked to my motel room. He claimed it was because he had an early morning ahead. Really, I think he worried we'd lose control.

"Okay." I sat up, but instead of standing and collecting my trash from dinner, I came down on top of him, pressing my chest to his. My lips brushed his mouth, placing a kiss at the corner.

He groaned, bringing a hand to my hair. He threaded his fingers into the strands, then tightened his stinging grip.

"Brooks," I hissed, my core tightening. Pulling against his hold, I puckered my lips, trying to reach his. But he held me tight, keeping our mouths from touching.

"If you kiss me again, I'll fuck you on this rock."

My breath caught. "What if I want you to fuck me on this rock?"

"Not tonight."

"Tomorrow?" I cocked an eyebrow.

He laughed. "No."

"Then the day after."

"Maybe."

"I can work with maybe." I smiled and pushed up.

I took a few deep breaths, orienting myself to the real world and blinking the dizzy haze of lust away. When I went to stand, Brooks's hand was waiting.

He helped me down from the rock and then we walked across the grass. I'd followed his lead tonight and skipped shoes. The grass was a thick, soft carpet between my toes. The last time I remembered walking barefoot in grass was as a little kid, when my mom had taken me to a park on one of her rare sober days.

"Tomorrow?" I asked.

He nodded. "Tomorrow."

I stayed still, wondering if he'd kiss me good night. He never did. When we were off the rock, there was no kissing. The only exception had been that first kiss in the garage.

Was he nervous about someone seeing us together? Unless someone was looking for us or had parked in his driveway, we were fairly well hidden and private. The rock sat far enough away from the motel that not even a guest taking a stroll on the sidewalk would notice.

Maybe he was still concerned about Moira. I'd already told him I wasn't scared of his ex-wife. But I could see why he'd want to protect me from her jealousy.

Or maybe he didn't want to be seen with a woman whose stay in Summers was as short-lived as a shooting star against the midnight sky.

"Thanks for dinner."

He tipped his invisible hat. "Night, Londyn."

My cheeks flushed. He treated me like I was a queen. Thomas had tried to do the same, showering me with gifts and luxuries. But Brooks was different. All he'd bought me was takeout. But that tip of the hat made me feel respected —admired even.

Brooks remained where I'd left him as I crossed the lawn to the motel. Every time I glanced back, he was there. His shoulders had slumped. The smile on his face had dropped. He stood like a sullen statue.

Watching me walk away.

———

RESTLESS ENERGY INVADED my bones the next morning. I went about my normal routine, getting ready for the day before wandering to the office for an iced coffee and whatever pastry they had for purchase. Today's were blueberry crumb muffins—I ate two.

The past few days, I'd entertained myself by reading. I'd wander to a park about six blocks away, take up a bench and disappear into a fictional world. Meggie had let me borrow her stack of tattered thrillers and I'd already devoured two. They were the perfect distraction to keep me from watching the clock, counting down the minutes until dinner with Brooks.

But today, as I stared at the words on the cream page, I couldn't make any of them connect. After reading the same paragraph three times, I tossed the book aside and flopped onto my bench. I stared at the blue sky without focusing, much like I had at my ceiling last night after leaving Brooks on the lawn.

The image of him standing stoically as I walked away had haunted my sleep.

Except he wasn't on a lawn, but a sidewalk. And I was looking at him through my rearview mirror.

Just over a week ago, I'd been more excited about this trip to California than I'd been about anything in years. I'd been energized by the open road. I'd been at peace driving the Cadillac. And I'd been happily anxious at the prospect of seeing Karson's face after all this time.

I still wanted to get to California, didn't I? *Yes.* But not with the same desperation I'd had a week ago. I was embracing my days here, holding nothing back.

A flat tire and Brooks Cohen had thwarted my plans. His long, wet kisses and the slow strokes of his tongue had taken priority over my road trip.

The dull throb in my center pulsed. This anticipation was torture. Delicious, excruciating torture. Would tonight be the night? Would either of us be able to stop at a kiss?

My fingers fidgeted on my stomach. My feet tapped on the bench.

I sat up and slid on my flip-flops, hoping the walk back to the motel under the shade of the serene trees would settle some of this anxiety.

It didn't. I was still flustered, brimming with sexual tension, when my temporary home came into view.

The parking lot of the motel was busier than it had been earlier. Inside the office, most of the chairs were taken, the local crew enjoying their midmorning coffee and gossip.

The warm and humid morning air filled my lungs. I'd be begging for the air conditioning later in the day, but no matter how hot and muggy it got by dinner, I wasn't missing time on that rock with Brooks.

It hadn't been bad the past few nights, but I was considerably stickier than I had been other mornings this week. Meggie had mentioned something about a heat wave coming. If it was too hot, maybe Brooks would invite me into his house tonight. Or I could invite him into my room for a motel picnic.

Thinking about the two of us kissing on a bed wasn't helping the tightening ache in my core.

"Londyn."

That voice was an ice bucket dumped over my head. I turned slowly on the sidewalk and came face-to-face with my ex-husband.

Goddamn it. I should have known he wouldn't let our last phone call be the end.

Thomas strode over from a black sedan with tinted windows. His dark hair didn't move as he walked. It was trimmed short except for the stylish swoop on top. Only when he was close could I make out the grays threaded through his temples.

"What are you doing here?" I fisted my hands on my hips. "And how did you find me?"

He frowned, looking me up and down. I was in a pair of boyfriend jeans, the holes at the knees bigger than a baseball. "I'm glad to see you're all right."

I was more than all right. Or I had been before he'd shown up. "Answer me. How did you find me, and what are you doing here?"

Thomas narrowed his boring, betraying brown eyes. "When you didn't return my calls, I reached out to Gemma."

"I heard."

Thomas's mouth thinned into an annoying line. "You found the time to call her but couldn't let me know you were alive."

"She's my friend. You are not." What the hell did he expect? We were divorced. And there was no way I was keeping in touch to see if junior was a boy or a girl.

"She mentioned you didn't take your phone."

"Nope."

He cringed. Thomas hated the word *nope*. He hated

the word *yep*. When we'd been married, I'd used *yes* or *no* in place of their more casual counterparts so as not to irritate him.

"Londyn, be reasonable." He pinched the bridge of his nose. "We need to be able to get in touch with you."

"For what? And you still haven't answered my question. How did you find me?" Even Gemma didn't know I was in West Virginia.

"You left me no choice."

Ah, yes. This was my fault. "Uh-huh."

"I hired a private investigator."

My body went rigid and I stood taller. Thomas was tall, standing just over six feet. He had inches on me and a lot of bulk. He'd always kept in shape by running and lifting weights at our home gym. But as I straightened, he went back on his heels.

"That is a gross invasion of my privacy, Thomas." I poked a finger into his chest.

"What was I supposed to do, Londyn? Let my ex-wife drive across the country?"

"Yes!" I threw up my hands.

"I'm try—"

"Everything all right here?" Brooks's deep voice sank into my bones as he stepped up to my side.

"It's fine." Thomas waved Brooks along. "We're having a private conversation."

"What are you doing here?" I looked up at Brooks. Shouldn't he be at work already?

"I had a tow call at six this morning. Once I got the car to the shop, I came home to shower and get some coffee."

The strands of his golden hair were loose and damp. My fingers itched to dive in and twist a lock around my finger.

"You know each other?" Thomas narrowed his eyes as he looked between us.

"Yep." I smiled as he cringed again.

"Here." Thomas dug into the pockets of his slacks. They were navy and the seam was perfectly creased down the center. He'd probably flown to the airport and rented that sedan this morning. From his pocket, he pulled out a phone.

My phone, to be exact.

"How did you get that? I gave it to Gemma." And she never would have given it to him.

"My PI retrieved it for me."

"What?" I shrieked. "You mean he stole it from her."

Thomas shrugged, shaking the phone at me. "I need to be able to reach you."

"For what?" I swiped the phone from his grip and immediately threw it on the sidewalk. The screen didn't even crack. Damn it.

"Londyn, what the fuck?" Thomas bent for the phone but it was too late.

I raised my knee above my waist and brought my heel down onto the phone. The screen cracked, but it wasn't the utter destruction I'd been after. So I tried again, still not achieving total annihilation and now my heel hurt. Flip-flops weren't exactly practical for phone obliteration.

"Grr." I stomped again, no doubt looking like a toddler having a tantrum, only to catch the edge of the phone.

"Let me." Brooks took my elbow, easing me aside. Then with one step, he shattered my phone to pieces.

"Ha!" I giggled. "Thanks. I should have done that in Boston."

"Anytime." He smiled.

Thomas stared at us both, his mouth agape.

"Was there something else you needed, Thomas? I imagine Secretary would prefer it if you scurried back to the city. Does she know you're stalking your ex-wife? Oh, and should I start referring to her as Baby Mama now?"

"She was a mistake, Londyn. I made a mistake."

"So did I," I admitted. "Somewhere along the way, I forgot who I was."

"And you've remembered?"

I'd run away from home to find a better life all those years ago. I was doing the same now. "I'm not coming back to Boston, Thomas. That part of my life is over."

He stared at me for a long moment. His silence grew and stretched until the heat surrounded us, making it uncomfortably hot. Beside me, Brooks stood perfectly still. Most men would leave me here alone with Thomas, not wanting to intrude on a personal conversation.

Not Brooks.

He was here as the protector. The man who'd already

bought me a phone, not stolen the one I'd chosen to leave behind. He wouldn't leave me alone with Thomas, maybe because he sensed I didn't want him to go.

"I can't change your mind," Thomas said.

I shook my head. "No."

Thomas studied my face, his gaze drifting over my mouth and up my nose. Then across my forehead and down my cheek. What was he doing? Was he memorizing me?

Maybe he finally understood this was the end.

"Goodbye, Thomas."

"If you change your mind—"

"I won't."

He dropped his chin, then looked up with a familiar, hardened stare. That shrewd, calculating gaze I'd seen so often at his office was fixed firmly in place. Without another word, Thomas shot a glare at Brooks, then strode to his car.

I held my breath, waiting until the vehicle's red taillights flashed and sped away from the curb. Then when I blew out all the air from my lungs, the weight of our divorce lifted.

Done. It was finally done.

My foot bumped the broken phone on the concrete. I bent and picked up the shattered pieces.

"So that's the ex?" Brooks asked.

"That's him."

"I'm starting to see why you ran away."

I smiled. "We weren't a good fit. I tried to fit into his life for a while, but . . ."

"You need to be free."

How was it that a man I'd known for a week knew me better than the man I'd lived with for years? This stunning, bold man saw me for who I was, not who I'd been pretending to be.

I'd tried so hard to fit into Thomas's life. But we were from different worlds. Thomas wore his wealth like a second skin. Even today, dressed in slacks and a light blue dress shirt, he exuded a level of class that was in his blood. He'd gone to a private school and his family spent Christmas in Fiji. His first car had been a Mercedes. He had two private planes.

I didn't want to fit into that world, where I was expected to act and speak a certain way.

I needed to be free.

"Thanks." I smiled at Brooks, admiring his clean-shaven face.

"For what?"

"For getting it. Not many do."

The corner of his mouth turned up. "You're one of a kind, Londyn McCormack. I've never met another person like you."

Thomas had said something similar when we'd met. Yet he'd tried to change me anyway. And shame on me, I'd let him. But not Brooks. He said those words with so much appreciation, I had a hard time breathing.

"Still on for dinner?" he asked.

I nodded, unable to speak.

Then he bent and kissed my cheek. Right there on the sidewalk in broad daylight with the entire congregation inside the motel's office bearing witness. Had he known I'd been feeling insecure? Most likely. Brooks seemed to understand me better than anyone ever had, including Karson.

Brooks left me on the sidewalk, crossing his lawn to where his truck was parked outside his garage. I stayed put —this time I had to watch him walk away.

My shoulders slumped. My smile dropped.

I didn't like it.

CHAPTER NINE

BROOKS

I used my forearm to wipe the sweat from my forehead, then slammed the hood on the truck I'd just finished working on. It was the Chevy I'd hauled in early yesterday morning. The owner hadn't been able to get it to start. When I'd gotten it into the shop, I'd understood why. The thing hadn't been tuned up in years. The oil was practically sludge and the battery corroded. The starter was on its last leg.

The owner was new to Summers and had recently moved into the widow Aster's place after she passed in March. He'd given me the go-ahead to fix it all, so after getting parts yesterday and clearing the shop, today it had been my project.

"Chevy's done," I told Tony, wiping my forehead again. The sweat wouldn't stop dripping. "You can go ahead and call for him to pick it up."

"Will do, Brooks." Tony unscrewed the cap on a gallon jug of water and hefted it to his lips. Most of the water went inside his mouth, but a healthy trickle dripped down his chin and onto his coveralls.

No matter the temperature, Tony wore coveralls. Today, he'd at least given up hot coffee for cold water.

"What else we got on the docket for the day?" Tony asked, catching a dribble of water with his wrist.

I blew out a long breath and stared down the shop to the office. "I need to spend some hours on paperwork."

I hadn't sent invoices in a week, and as much as I hated keeping the books, I did like getting paid. Normally, I did my billing at night. I'd stick around after the shop closed. Unless Wyatt had a night off or we had Monday dinner at Mom and Dad's house, I was here until my growling stomach forced me home.

Those three or four nights a week made it possible for me to keep up on the business side of things. But with Londyn here, I'd left every night this week as soon as the last car was out of the shop and on the road with its owner.

Last night, I'd even closed up early. I'd hoped to catch Wyatt between football practice and work so I could tell him about Londyn. But he'd had a friend over when I'd gotten home, so I'd put it off. As soon as he'd gone to work, I'd hauled ass to the diner to pick up a couple of cheese-burgers, then met Londyn on the rock.

I'd been braced for her to be in an off mood thanks to her ex's visit. But she'd been her normal self when she'd shown up to meet me. We'd talked about her life over dinner. Londyn had quickly become my favorite topic. I'd asked her more questions about the journey from California to Montana to Boston and the places she'd stopped along the way.

By the time our cheeseburgers had been devoured, the pair of us had been too full to do anything but lie on the rock and watch the sunset with our hands linked.

As much as I would have liked kissing her for an hour, my lips were chapped and my control on the brink. One taste of her and I wouldn't have had the strength to stop at a kiss.

It was killing me to send her on her way to the motel each night. Alone. I'd walked stiffly home, my cock so swollen and aching I'd been forced to take a miserably long cold shower.

At the moment, a cold shower sounded great. I was melting, and just thinking about Londyn had stirred my dick to life.

The last time I'd been this hot for a woman had been . . . never. Not even as a teenager with Moira. And I was about done waiting. I'd been patient, but there was only so much a man could take.

I glanced at the clock. It was nearly noon. Tony had come in early this morning, around six according to his punch card. I'd been in shortly after eight, having hung around the house this morning to make sure Wyatt had breakfast before leaving for practice.

He was a zombie in the mornings. During the school year, both Moira and I made sure he was out of bed because he could sleep through ten blaring alarms. I'd hoped today might be the exception to his normal dazed routine so I could tell him about Londyn. But he'd nearly fallen asleep in his eggs.

I'd kept the conversation light, talking about football and his plans for a summer Friday night. He'd woken up enough to ask if he could take a girl to the movies. I'd agreed as long as he promised to spend some much-needed time with his old man on the boat tomorrow.

"I'm ready for the weekend," I told Tony.

"Same. You got plans?" He raised an eyebrow, no doubt wondering if I had plans with Londyn. Though he hadn't outright asked about her, it was no secret that I'd had dinner with her every night this week.

Meggie knew it. Therefore, Sally knew it. Therefore, Tony and the whole town knew it.

"Wyatt and I'll probably take the boat out."

"Good plan." He fanned his face. "This heat sure came on fast."

That was no joke. Another reason all Londyn had gotten last night was a chaste kiss good night. It was too damn hot to get worked up.

The worst of the summer heat had descended on Summers and would stick around until September. The days would be sticky, the nights muggy and thick. I needed to find time to tell Wyatt about Londyn and fast, because the rock wasn't going to be enjoyable again until fall. My back porch was much more comfortable—so was my bed.

"Tony?" I glanced around the empty shop. We were done with jobs for the day. "I think I'm going to spend the rest of the day in my office. You should take the afternoon off."

"Yeah?" He swiped up his gallon of water from the tool bench. "Think I'll take you up on that."

"Good. Have a nice weekend." I waved as he headed for the door.

"You too, Brooks."

I retreated to the office, sinking down in the chair and enjoying the slightly cooler air. The ceiling vent blew air into my face.

I closed my eyes, giving myself ten minutes to cool down and work up the gumption to open my laptop. But I didn't get ten minutes. I only got three before a rap came at the door. My eyes shot open to a beautiful sight.

Londyn leaned against the doorframe with a smile. A pair of denim shorts left most of her legs bare. Her green tank top dipped dangerously low in a scoop around her neck, the color bringing out the darker greens in her eyes. "Did I interrupt nap time?"

I waved her into the room toward the chair in the corner. "It's the heat. I needed a breather."

"Seriously." She fanned her face. "Someone turned up the dial because it's miserable."

"To what do I owe the pleasure?"

She relaxed deeper into the chair. "I'm bored. It's too hot to walk around town and I couldn't stay cramped up in my motel room any longer."

Londyn was growing restless. Soon, she'd be gone. "Got a call from the body shop today. They're starting on your car first thing Monday. Should be done by Friday at the latest."

"A week." She sighed.

"Is that too long? I can ask if they can hurry it." Maybe if I asked Mack, he'd be willing to work the weekend for some extra cash.

"No." She toyed with the frayed hem of her shorts. "I was just thinking it was too soon."

"It is too soon." I grinned. If she wasn't in a hurry, maybe I could convince her to stay through next weekend too.

"Mind if I hang out here for a while?" she asked. "I promise to ask you a bunch of questions and distract you from getting any work done."

"Well, when you put it like that . . ."

"I'm kidding. Give me ten to cool down and then I'll get out of your hair."

"Nah. Stay as long as you want." Nothing I needed to do today was urgent. It could all wait until the weekend. Or next week. Or the week after that. I'd probably want the extra work after Londyn left town anyway. It would be a nice distraction.

She sank even deeper, resting her head on the back of

the leather chair. "What does a sexy mechanic do on a hot Friday afternoon in West Virginia?"

"Sexy?" I raised an eyebrow.

"Definitely sexy."

I chuckled. "Well, if that mechanic has a stack of bills to pay and invoices to send, he spends it in the office. If he's not in the mood to work and doesn't have a car to fix, he's out on the lake in his boat."

Londyn sat up straight. "You have a boat?"

"I do."

"Hmm. Interesting." She tapped her chin. "I happen to like boats."

Fuck the office. I stood from my chair and took my truck keys off the hook by the door. "Let's get out of here."

———

"I MIGHT HAVE INSISTED on dinner here if I'd known about it." Londyn stood at the end of my dock, staring down at my boat. "What else are you hiding from me?"

I held out my hand to help her into the boat. "Not a lot."

Only my teenager.

She smiled, her eyes hidden behind dark sunglasses as she took a seat in the passenger chair. She hadn't changed from the office. We'd driven over together and while I'd run into my house to swap my jeans and boots for board shorts and sandals, she'd wandered around the back of the house and found the dock.

"This is some place." She glanced back toward the house.

"It wasn't easy to come by, but I got lucky. My dad worked with the previous owner. She was a doctor at the hospital with him. She and her husband retired to Florida. Dad knew I was looking to buy and gave me the tip."

Lakefront homes with a private dock didn't appear on the market in Summers often. This one hadn't even been listed. We'd agreed upon a price, and when they'd moved out and I'd moved in, it was the talk of the town for weeks.

Some didn't like that they'd been cheated the opportunity to bid. If they knew how much I'd paid, they wouldn't be bitching. My offer had been three times as much as a house like this in town would cost. But the location had been worth taking a loan from my parents.

"Ready?" I asked and Londyn nodded.

I started up the boat, the rumble radiating from the engine through the floor. Then I eased us away from the dock, pointing the bow toward the center of the lake. When we were clear, I lowered the throttle.

Londyn's smile widened, her eyes aimed at the shore behind us as we flew. She pointed to the rock when she spotted it and laughed.

From the rock, the shoreline of the lake jutted out about thirty feet, hiding the dock from view. But out here, in the middle of the water, you could see how each landmark bookended my property line between my neighbor on one side and the motel on the other.

"This feels so good!" Londyn yelled above the rev of the engine and the slap of water against the hull.

The air rushed around us, creating the breeze we'd been missing. Her hair flew behind and around her face as she spun forward, watching where I was going.

We cruised, making the long lap around the lake. There were a few other boats out on the water today, all fishermen bobbing along the banks at slow speeds, and we waved as we passed them by. Tomorrow the lake would be packed, everyone out to enjoy the weekend and beat the heat.

I brought us to the center of the lake, to a spot where we'd have some privacy, and shut off the boat. No one would bother us out here. The fishermen were working the edges and coves where the walleye and smallmouth bass were searching for food.

"Thank you for this." Londyn slid her sunglasses into that long, blond hair, revealing those shining jade eyes.

My mouth went dry. "Water. Need one?" I sure as hell did. My head was dizzy and my heart was beating in hard *thunks*. The heat was getting to me again—I was burning up, from the inside out.

"I was thinking of going for a swim."

Thunk. "Didn't think you had a suit."

There was no tie at the nape of her neck. She hadn't gone to the motel to change after coming to the office.

"Do I need one?"

Thunk. "Uh, no."

She gave me a sly grin, one that said she was ten steps ahead and I'd better catch up fast. Her tank top was gone in a flash of cotton, leaving nothing but skin and black lace cupping perfect breasts. Londyn looked up at me through her lashes as her fingers trailed down the flat line of her stomach to the waistband on her denim shorts.

Those slim, lithe fingers flicked open the button. The zipper clicked, one notch at a time, until her hands slid toward her hips to push the shorts down her legs. She shimmied, a gentle sway, until all that was left was black lace.

"Are you swimming with me?" She stepped out of her sandals and walked to the back of the boat, stepping up on the bench seat, then the rear deck. Her toes wiggled forward until they were gripping the edge, ready to catapult her into the water.

I managed a nod.

Then she was off, the dive graceful and smooth, like the woman herself. The stunning woman who'd swept into my life and captured my attention like no other.

Thunk.

My hand pressed against my heart. She was stealing it, little by little.

"Are you coming in here?" she hollered from the water after popping up about twenty feet away. "Or are you afraid of a woman swimming in her underwear?"

136

"Smart-ass." I grinned, reaching behind my head to yank off my T-shirt. My flip-flops were still under the steering wheel where I'd kicked them off during the drive. Three long strides and I was up and off the boat, stretching long as I dove into the water.

Surfacing beside her, I slicked the hair off my face. "What was that about your underwear?"

Londyn smiled, her hands coming to my shoulders as she drifted closer. Her legs tangled with mine in the cool water below as we treaded to keep afloat.

I wrapped one arm around her waist, pulling her hips flush against the ridges of my stomach. With my other hand, I cupped her ass, squeezing the wet lace in my palm. She gasped when I pressed my erection into her inner thigh.

"You're driving me crazy, honey."

She leaned in, her lips a whisper from mine. "If you kiss me today, you'd better not stop."

There'd be no stopping, not today. I'd threatened to fuck her on that rock, but the boat would work fine instead.

My lips crashed into hers, the sweet taste of her mouth consuming me as my tongue dove inside. I pulled her closer with one arm, holding tight as I plundered her mouth and my other hand stretched for the boat, using it to keep my balance as my legs propelled us.

"Brooks," she panted my name, breaking her lips away when we reached the boat's platform.

"Up." I put my hands on her hips, hoisting her out of the water. Drops fell from her tan skin, landing on me as I planted my hands on the platform and shoved myself out of the water. The moment my feet were steady, she was in my arms, our bodies crashing together and our mouths fusing.

We fumbled over the back of the boat, slipping and sliding as we made our way to the center aisle. I swiped a towel from the stack I'd brought along, shaking it out with one hand. I tore my lips away, making Londyn moan as I laid the towel on the wet carpet.

I took her hand, tugging her to her knees beside me. Then I wrapped her in my arms and eased her to the floor, hovering above her.

"This okay?"

She nodded, snaking a hand around my neck and pulling me down.

There was nothing languid or slow about our next kiss. This wasn't a kiss to explore or learn about one another. This kiss was the prelude. This kiss was the last one in a long line of kisses that had led us here, to my bare chest against her smooth skin.

My hand reached between us, cupping her breast. I pulled the cup of her bra under the curve to set her nipple free. I twisted the hard nub in my hand, rolling it to a peak as her back arched off the towel.

I needed it in my mouth. I needed to taste every inch

of this incredible woman. I tore my lips away, dropping to suck on her skin.

"*Shit*," she hissed, her fingers diving into the wet strands of my hair as I rolled her nipple around my tongue. Her eyelids were closed, her wet mouth open as she breathed.

She was a picture of ecstasy and we hadn't even gotten to the good parts yet.

I grinned, giving her nipple a playful nip before leaning away and stripping the straps of her bra off her shoulders. It closed in the back so she pushed up, reaching behind to undo the clasp.

"Condom?" Her chest heaved. "Please tell me you have a condom on this boat."

"Yeah." I popped open the compartment below the steering wheel and retrieved my wallet. I'd put a condom in there earlier this week, just in case my control cracked.

With the foil packet in my hand, I tossed the wallet aside and ripped at Londyn's panties. The lace shredded as I tugged hard, and the scrap of fabric got tossed carelessly to the side.

Londyn relaxed onto her elbows, her eyes hooded as she widened her legs.

My hand went to my heart once more. "You're . . ." My heart did another *thunk*. "Beautiful."

That wasn't the right word but as a smile spread across her face, I lost the ability to think.

Her eyes darted to my shorts. "Are you going to take those off? Or would you like some help?"

"Don't. Move."

I stood and ripped the wet shorts off my legs. My erection bobbed, throbbing hard as she spread even wider. I tore into the condom, sheathing myself, and when it was in place, my eyes dropped to her bare, slick pussy.

Fuck. I wasn't going to last. My stamina was shit and she deserved more than a fifteen-minute ride.

"Brooks." She squirmed. "If you don't get down here—"

I dove on her, not letting my insecurities win out. I slammed my mouth onto hers—fuck the stamina. Today we'd scratch the itch. Tonight, the next night and the night after that, I'd worship her body until she came apart, over and over again.

Gripping my cock, I rubbed the tip through her folds. The shudder that ran through her vibrated against my skin and she arched, her hips circling as she searched for more. I positioned myself at the entrance, pausing and taking a long breath to get myself in check. Then I rocked inside an inch, Londyn's body so tight and hot I squeezed my eyes shut.

"Oh, God," she moaned. Her hands came up to my chest and her nails dug into my pecs.

My hips drove me deeper, the pulse of her inner muscles clamping down tight. I let her adjust around me and pressed forward. I inched inside, slowly and deliberately, until the base of my cock was rooted against her flesh.

"Fuck, you feel so good." I dropped my forehead to hers, giving myself another moment.

"I'm—" Her breath fluttered as her hips rolled. "More."

I obeyed, working myself in and out. The pace started slow but picked up quickly until each time I thrust inside, our bodies smacked together and her breasts shook. I held myself above her, my stomach taut as I used every ounce of strength to keep the explosion coming at bay.

My hand drifted between us, my finger finding her clit. The minute I grazed it, she about came off the floor.

"Brooks," she gasped. One more brush was all it took and her whole body shuddered, coming apart. She writhed, riding out the orgasm with a series of moans and breaths that was heaven in my ears.

She clenched around me, and the pressure at the base of my spine was too much to shove away. I came on the heels of her climax, her name on my lips.

When I recovered and the white spots in my vision cleared, I slid out and disposed of the condom in a sack I'd brought for trash. My body was damp with sweat and the water from the lake.

There was barely enough room to collapse beside her, but we both shifted onto our sides as she let me thread my arm behind her head.

I kissed her temple and wet hair. "Damn, honey."

"That was . . ." She gulped. "Wow."

"You comfortable?"

She snuggled into my bare chest and nodded.

We lay there, hot and sweaty and naked, shielded from the sun, as we looked into the open blue sky above. The boat rocked us back and forth. The water lapped against its sides.

A week. I had a week with this woman, maybe nine or ten days, to soak her in. Then I'd let her go, already knowing that watching her drive away was going to hurt like a son of a bitch.

CHAPTER TEN

LONDYN

The moment the knock sounded, I leapt off the bed and rushed for the knob. I didn't bother checking the peephole—Brooks knocked with the same three short taps each night.

"Hey." Brooks grinned as I yanked the door open.

"Hi." I grabbed a fistful of his T-shirt and dragged him inside.

His mouth descended on mine as he kicked the door shut. We were a mess of hands and lips as he walked me backward to the bed, lifting me up by the ribs to lay me on the mattress.

"What took you so long?" I breathed as he kissed his way down my neck.

He broke away to glance at the clock on the night-stand, his forehead furrowing. "I'm two minutes late."

"Exactly." I pulled at the hem of his shirt, tugging it up his back. "I've been waiting forever."

He rolled his eyes as he yanked off the shirt the rest of the way. "You could have saved us some time and answered the door naked."

I giggled. "Tomorrow."

"Promise?"

I nodded, reaching between us for the button on his jeans.

This was the third night of our motel-room rendezvouses, and the dance to rid one another of clothing took less and less time each night. Practice makes progress.

I hadn't spent the day with Brooks since our boat ride on Friday. He'd been busy all weekend and unable to spend time with me during the day.

I'd done my best not to spy. The window in my room overlooked the backside of the motel, out toward the lake and not his yard. But I'd gone out of my room and wandered some. Each time, his truck had been missing from the driveway in his house. Okay, I'd spied.

But he'd come to my room each night and stayed for five or six hours, long enough that I was boneless by the time he left to walk home in the dark. Eating dinner and making out on the rock had been replaced with hot, wild and sweaty sex. A fair trade.

I worked the zipper on Brooks's jeans free, diving in to wrap my hand around his shaft.

He bit my lip as I squeezed. "Naughty woman."

That bite was just the beginning. We teased and tormented one another until I was a writhing, screaming mess, pinned to the bed with my hands above my head and his body driving me to the edge.

After we came apart, he flopped beside me, that glorious, broad chest heaving. I slid my fingers into the dusting of dark hair across it, resting my palm over his hard nipple.

"I shouldn't have worked out today," he breathed.

I turned sideways, propping my head on an elbow. "You worked out?"

He nodded. "I went for a run this morning before going to the garage."

"In this heat?" Wild horses couldn't have dragged me on a run in this humidity. He should have come here instead; I would have worked him out. "Do you normally run?"

"Hold that question." He bent and stood from the bed, giving me a moment to appreciate his firm ass and the strength in his back as he walked to the bathroom. It didn't take him long to dispose of the condom and return to the bed, the view of the front just as gorgeous as the back.

He mirrored my position, lying on a side to face me, and flicked the sheet over our legs and hips. "I need to tell you something."

My body tensed. The last time I'd heard those words, Gemma had informed me that Secretary was pregnant.

"It's not bad." He grinned, using his free hand to rub away the crease between my eyebrows.

"Okay." I relaxed a bit.

"The reason I ran this morning was because my son asked me to go with him."

"Your son?" I blinked, replaying the word. "You have a son?"

Brooks nodded. "I have a son. He's sixteen. He shares time between my house and Moira's. Last week, he was with her. This week, he's with me."

"Ah." That explained why he'd been absent all weekend. It stung that in all our conversations, I hadn't learned about his son. "Why didn't you tell me about him?"

"It wasn't because I was trying to hide him from you." Brooks took my hand and laced our fingers together. "I didn't want you to know about him and him not know about you, if that makes sense."

"It does. You put him first." A foreign concept to my own parents. Had anyone in my life ever put me first? I couldn't think of a single person, not even Thomas. Only if it served him had he made me a priority.

That Brooks put his son above anyone else endeared him to me even more.

A single dad. A *good*, single dad. This man kept getting better.

"What's his name?" I asked.

"Wyatt."

"The Thai delivery boy?"

Brooks chuckled. "Yeah. He actually does deliveries for a few restaurants in town, not just the Thai place."

"Oh. Is that where he is tonight?"

"No, he's home. We have a standing dinner date with my parents on Monday nights. Last week, I begged out of it to meet you at the diner for pie. But Wyatt and I both went tonight. Then we came home. He's at the house, texting some girl."

"And you came to me."

He tucked a lock of hair behind my ear. "I came to you."

I saw it now, the resemblance between father and son. When Wyatt had been in the motel lobby, I hadn't put it together because, well . . . why would I? But now that I could pair them together, I saw how Wyatt had Brooks's nose and the promise of the same strong build.

"Does he know about me?"

Brooks nodded. "He does."

I didn't need to ask how Wyatt felt about Brooks seeing a woman living at the motel. If his son had a problem with me, Brooks would have already said goodbye.

"When did you tell him?" I asked.

"This weekend. I told him I was enamored with one of my customers."

"Enamored?"

"Completely." He rolled across the distance between us, his bare chest pressing mine into the bed. "I'm sorry for not telling you about him sooner."

Time seemed to have slowed in Summers. It seemed

like Brooks and I had been together for a long time, when in reality, it had been less than two weeks. Standing in his shoes, I wouldn't have brought Wyatt into the conversation early either. Brooks the protector had waited until it was the right time to share.

A jolt of pride hit my heart. Brooks had deemed me worth sharing. He could have kept us quiet. I'd be gone soon. But he'd shared me with his son.

"I understand."

"You do?"

I nodded, studying the smooth skin on his cheek. He must have shaved before dinner with his parents. I ran my knuckles up his jaw toward his temple. There were no grays threaded through his dark blond hair. "How old are you?"

"Thirty-three."

My eyes widened. "And you have a sixteen-year-old son?"

"Yeah. Wyatt was born when I was seventeen."

"Wow."

I'd become a parent to myself when I was sixteen. He'd become an actual parent at seventeen. There was no question that his youth had been harder. It also made sense why we connected so well when other men close to my age often seemed so immature.

Circumstances had forced us both to grow up fast.

"You had a short childhood too."

He studied my face, his eyes softening. "Yeah. But I

don't regret it for a minute. Things were hard for a few years, but I had help. I had more support than you did, that's for sure. My parents. Moira's too."

Moira was Wyatt's mother. Was that why she'd acted out against my car? Because she saw me as a threat to not only her ex-husband, but her son's father too? "When did you get married?"

"As soon as we turned eighteen." Brooks dropped his head to the bed, lying close so we could look at one another. Between us, he kept his grip on my hand. "Moira and I tried, for Wyatt. But it got too hard, and I didn't want my son growing up thinking that was what a marriage should be. We didn't laugh. We didn't talk to one another. We just . . . existed."

That sounded familiar. "How long ago did you get divorced?"

"Ten years. You?"

I hesitated. It felt like longer, but in reality, it had been only six months since I'd caught Thomas with Secretary. "Officially, three weeks."

"Oh." Brooks's gaze dropped to the pillow, his grip on my hand loosening. "Three weeks. That's, uh . . . three weeks."

No time at all, unless you knew my heart. Then you'd know that those three weeks were more than enough to say goodbye to my marriage. The moment I'd found Thomas with his dick inside a moaning Secretary, I'd fallen out of love with him. I'd had months during the divorce proceedings and settlement to make peace with the end.

I'd changed my last name. I'd arranged to leave the home we'd shared. Running away hadn't been hard at all.

Brooks ran his free hand over his jaw. "This is probably a week too late, but is this a rebound thing? Or some step you have to take to get over your ex?"

"Never." I shifted up to meet his eyes. "You're not a rebound."

"You sure about that?"

I cupped his cheek. "I'm not spending time with you, having sex with you, because I'm here to prove to my ex-husband that I've moved on. I'm not having sex with you because I need to prove to myself that I've moved on. I'm having sex with you because you're an amazing kisser, your hands feel like a dream on my body and, in case you haven't noticed, I'm enamored with you too."

Brooks grinned, relief washing over us both. "Tell me something else about you."

"Like what?"

"I don't know. Anything."

I dropped to his side, stretching a leg across his as I curled into his chest. His arm wrapped around my shoulders to trap me close.

If tonight was anything like last night and the night before that, we'd lie here talking for a while before one of us would make a move. It didn't take much to ignite the simmering heat—a touch on my breast, a graze along his thigh, a whisper in my ear. But first, we'd talk.

The question game we'd started on the rock had been intended as a two-way street. Except each night, I found myself talking more about me than Brooks did about himself. Was that because he'd been trying to keep Wyatt from entering the mix? Or had I taken over our conversations, unintentionally keeping the focus on myself?

I was leaving so many stories behind but only taking a few of his with me on my journey.

"Why do we always talk about me?" I asked.

"Because I want to learn it all, and I'm running out of time."

We were running out of time. "Is my car still on track to be done Friday?"

"Far as I know."

Even if I stayed through the weekend, by this time next week, I'd be gone.

Maybe it was easier to keep talking about me. The more I learned about Brooks, the harder it was to imagine leaving him behind. I'd known everything there was to know about Thomas, and I hadn't thought twice about running from Boston.

My stomach tightened, the anxiety of that day growing. Driving away from Summers would be a hundred times more difficult than leaving Boston. Necessary, but agonizing.

"You said the car was going to a friend in California. Who?" he asked.

"His name is Karson."

"He?"

I liked the hint of jealousy in his voice, not that there was any reason to be jealous. Karson was only a fond memory. "Karson was a runaway too. He lived in the junk-yard—actually, he was the one who discovered it in the first place."

Karson had been wandering around Temecula, searching for a bench or some place to sleep one night. When he hadn't found anything to his liking, he'd kept walking until he'd spotted a fire.

The old man who managed the junkyard had been burning some wood scraps in a barrel. The light had caught Karson's attention and he'd snuck in, sleeping under the stars on a foam bench seat that had once been in a truck.

"He'd been living there for a month before the owner of the yard finally came out one night with a blanket. Lou Miley was his name, the junkyard owner."

Speaking his name brought a smile to my lips. The last time I'd spoken to Lou had been when I'd called to buy the Cadillac. He'd sounded the same as ever. Gruff and grumpy. He spoke in grunts whenever possible. Lou was a naturally unhappy soul, annoyed by the mainstream world. But for us kids, he'd opened his heart. He'd been our hero.

Lou was gone now. Three months after I'd bought the Cadillac, Gemma had gotten word that he'd died in his sleep. Lou hadn't socialized much, but I knew of six people who would have mourned his passing, me included.

"So how'd you meet Karson?"

"Gemma," I said. "They lived in the same trailer park. When he stopped coming home after school, she knew he was gone. Then when she ran, she asked around until she found him. He set her up at the junkyard too. Then she found me a month later and two became three."

I'd been digging through the trash behind a restaurant for food. She'd slapped a sandwich out of my hand, rolled her eyes and ordered me to follow her. She'd taken me to the junkyard, shared some of her food stash and introduced me to Karson.

"Three." Brooks drummed the number on my lower back. "I thought you said there were six of you kids."

"It was only the three of us for about two months. Then Katherine came along. She met Karson at the car wash where he worked. Then came Aria and Clara. Those two were my recruits."

It sounded strange to say recruits. Most parents would frown at the idea of one kid talking another into running away from home. But home wasn't always a loving term. Sometimes home meant pain and fear. Home was what we'd been seeking to escape.

"Where'd you find them?" Brooks asked. There was no

judgment in his voice. The shock of my life's history had faded since our first night together. He'd become more curious instead. He'd accepted that running away had been the best of a long list of shitty options.

It had been for Aria and Clara too.

"They found me. They lived two trailers down from my parents with their uncle. When they were ten, their parents died in a car accident. The uncle, he was . . . not right. You know how you can see someone from a distance and you get that shiver up your spine? That was him. Aria and Clara didn't tell me much about why they left, but they didn't need to. They walked into the junkyard one day and never looked back."

I could still picture the twins walking hand in hand into the junkyard like they owned the place. They'd heard from some kids at the pizza parlor where I'd worked that it was where I'd been *hanging out.*

We didn't tell people, even other kids, we actually lived there for fear the police would show up and take us home.

"So Karson is in California—"

"Maybe," I said. "I actually don't know if Karson is still there. Gemma got word a couple years back that he still lived in Temecula—he was at Lou's funeral—but he might have moved since."

"That's why you're going there first. To see if he's there."

"Yes. Maybe the others are too, I don't know.

Katherine could be in Montana where Gemma and I left her. Aria and Clara were a year younger than me and they stayed in the junkyard when we left. As far as I know, Karson stayed with them."

"If he's not there?"

I shrugged. "I'll find him. California is just my starting point."

I'd track Karson down and give him the car. Our car.

"We lived together in the Cadillac," I told Brooks. "That's why I want to give it to him. It was as much his as mine."

"Where did everyone else live? In other cars?"

I shifted to put my chin on his chest and meet his eyes. "No. There weren't many cars still intact. Mostly it was a graveyard of rusted pieces and parts. Gemma built herself a tent. It started as this little hut she built out of sheet metal, then it grew and grew. Sort of like the empire she's built in Boston."

"What does she do?" Brooks asked, his fingers drifting into my hair as I spoke.

"She started out selling real estate. Then she took the money she made and created a cosmetics line. From there, she got into fashion. Then she bought into a car dealership. She's a silent partner in three of Boston's finest restaurants. She has this gift. She takes one dollar and turns it into ten."

Thomas didn't like Gemma, mostly because he was jealous. At her rate, she'd surpass him in wealth within the next five years. I only hoped she found some happiness outside of work. I didn't want a work-driven life for my friend.

I wished to see her laugh more, like we had in those early days together.

But whatever she was searching for, she hadn't found it yet.

Neither had I.

"Her tent was the common area for us." I smiled, remembering us all sitting cross-legged in the center of her tent as we played poker, bidding with toothpicks instead of chips. "She found these tarps and created different spaces. Katherine stayed in the tent with Gemma. Aria and Clara made their home in the shell of a broken delivery truck."

It had been bigger than the Cadillac, but Karson and I had teased them relentlessly that our car had style while theirs was a white box.

"Were you and Karson . . ."

"A couple?" I asked and Brooks nodded. "Yes. For a short time."

Besides Gemma, Karson was the first person I'd truly loved. He was the first person who'd shown me what it felt like to *be* loved. The memory of that childhood crush was everlasting.

"We ended it when I left with Gemma and Katherine for Montana. We both knew a long-distance relationship at our age wasn't going to last. I lost touch with him, but I've always been curious how his life turned out."

Brooks hummed. "I guess you'll find out soon enough."

"I just hope I find him well." It would break my heart if Karson had lost the spark of the boy I'd loved. The boy who'd walked through life with charisma and confidence. He'd never looked at our situation with anything but excitement. Maybe that was why I considered those years an adventure. Karson had made that time magical.

He had for us all. He'd been the protector. The joke maker. The shoulder to cry on. Karson was the rock and the reason we'd all survived running away from home relatively unscathed.

"What if you don't find him?" Brooks asked.

"I'll find him." Somehow, I'd track him down. "I really want him to have the Cadillac."

"Why? You love that car."

"I do love that car. But I just feel like I've had it long enough. That it should belong to him too. Yes, I paid for it. But it doesn't feel . . . mine. Does that make any sense?"

Brooks was quiet for a long moment, then leaned up and kissed my forehead. "Yeah, honey. It does."

I pressed my cheek to his heart. It never took much explaining with Brooks. He knew how I felt even if I couldn't articulate it.

"So you'll go and find Karson and give him the car. Will you search for the others too?" he asked.

"Maybe."

I hadn't really thought that far ahead, my focus so much on first finding Karson.

It would be nice to see what had happened with their lives. When I found Karson, he might know where the others had gone. I'd thought about Katherine and Aria and Clara over the years. Were they happy? Had they battled their own demons and come out as victors?

"Yes," I whispered. "I think I would like to see them all again."

"Then I'm sure you will." Brooks rolled me off his shoulder and onto my back. He came up on top of me, brushing my hair off my face. "Stay. Just a little longer. Before you set off to find these people and I never see you again, stay. Give me two more weeks, not one."

Yes.

The word was right there. I opened my mouth to say it. But as I gazed into those bright blue eyes, it wouldn't come. What if I stayed and never left Summers? What if I regretted giving up my shot at freedom? What if I stayed and he broke my heart?

I couldn't stand to think of Brooks as another mistake. Not him.

Boston had never been my long-term plan. I'd gone there knowing I'd leave. But then I'd met Thomas. He'd asked me to stay too. Look where that had gotten me.

I wanted to say yes. *Damn it, I want to say yes.* Especially to Brooks. Which was exactly why the answer had to be—

"No."

CHAPTER ELEVEN

BROOKS

I hung up the phone, setting it on the boat's dashboard. "That was the body shop. Your car's done."

"Okay." Londyn kept her gaze on the water. "Do we have to go get it now? Or can we stay out here for a while?"

"We can stay."

We'd stay long enough for me to memorize how she looked today. Her hair was up, twisted in a knot, still wet from our swim. Sunglasses covered her eyes. The only thing she wore was a simple black bikini she'd bought at a local shop today when I'd invited her to spend the afternoon with me on the boat.

She was breathtaking. This was how I'd picture her in the years to come. I'd remember her sitting in that seat, soaking up the sun and stealing my heart with every passing second.

The week had gone by too fast.

That always seemed to be the case when the end drew near.

Mack had texted me earlier in the week, estimating he'd have Londyn's car done by Friday. Well, Friday was here, and true to his word, it was done. She'd be gone soon, which made my decision to take the day off work even smarter.

I'd called Tony this morning and asked if he could cover the garage. Fridays were typically busy but he'd assured me he'd take care of all the oil changes that rolled in. Worst-case scenario, he'd turn folks away for Monday. One Friday away wasn't going to sink my business. One missed day with Londyn would eat at me for years.

I'd gone over to her room first thing, before she disappeared on one of her walks around town, and asked her to spend the day with me. We'd gone to breakfast at the diner. We'd found her a swimming suit at Walmart. We'd loaded up on groceries for a picnic lunch. Then we'd headed for the water.

Much like the first time, I'd cruised us around the lake before coming to the middle to float. Then I'd stripped her out of that bikini and made love to her on the floor. We'd cooled off afterward with a swim. I'd just finished toweling off when my phone rang and Mack put a damper on my day.

She was leaving.

Fuck. Was I destined to be alone? Before Moira, there hadn't been many girls. Just a few high-school flings, forgotten before they'd even begun. Once Moira and I had hooked up, she'd made it known around Summers High that I was off-limits.

Our marriage had been doomed from the start. Moira and I had been opposites in every sense of the word—that old adage was bullshit. Opposites didn't attract. They annoyed.

After the divorce, after my failed attempts at dating, I'd decided I'd rather be single than with a woman more interested in my parents' money than me and my simple garage. Sure, I had a nice house and a new boat. I'd earned those things. I'd paid for them by working my ass off.

I had Wyatt. I had my family. I didn't feel alone.

Until Londyn.

She'd blown into town and made me realize the hole in my life. The hole in the exact shape of a five-foot-five blond woman with jade-green eyes.

Goddamn, I would miss her.

"It's really beautiful here." She smiled, casting her gaze at the trees that surrounded the lake. "I don't know if I'll ever find another lake as pretty as this one."

My heart. Replace *lake* with *woman* and she'd voiced the thoughts in my mind.

She'd been making comments like that all week, reminding us both she was leaving. How could I forget?

The minutes were ticking by too quickly. The nights I spent in her motel room weren't enough. We still had the weekend, but I needed more.

I wouldn't get more. I'd asked once.

I wouldn't ask again.

One *no* from this woman was enough to crush my hopes for good.

Londyn was leaving. I had no choice but to accept it, appreciate it even.

The longer she stayed, the more I'd keep begging for another day. I'd push for a week, then a month, then a year.

I was hungry for her in a way I'd never be full.

"Want to cruise around?" I asked.

"No." She turned away from the view and slid her sunglasses off her face. The emerald flecks in her eyes danced bright in the sunlight as she reached for the bikini tie behind her neck.

I grinned. *Hungry.*

———

WE SPENT the rest of the afternoon on the lake, exploring the water in between breaks from exploring each other. By late afternoon, the lake was teaming with boats, people out on the water for a few hours before dark to kick off the weekend. Neither Londyn nor I felt like being one in a crowd, so we called it a day.

The boat was tied to the dock and we were in my truck, driving to the garage to check out her car. Mack had done me a favor and brought it over so I didn't have to pick it up. Tony had texted that it was safely locked inside.

"Feel like dinner on the rock tonight?" Londyn asked.

"Or . . . we could eat at my place. With Wyatt."

She looked over, her eyebrows rising above her large sunglasses. "You want me to meet your son?"

"Haven't you already?"

"Well, yes. This is a bit different though, don't you think?"

"Not really. It's just you and me eating dinner with a kid who will probably be on his phone the whole time."

She pushed her sunglasses into her hair and shifted to face me. "Is that smart? I'm leaving on Monday."

"I know. But Wyatt knows about you. He knows you're leaving. He's my favorite person in the world. You're quickly climbing that list. For once, I've got two favorites in the same place. I'm trying to capitalize while I can."

She gave me a small smile. "I get that. How would you introduce me?"

"As a friend." Or a girlfriend. My son was no idiot. He knew where I'd been going each night.

Londyn thought it over for a minute, then nodded. "All right. As a friend."

Girlfriend.

"Pizza?" I steered us into the rear parking lot of the

garage where Tony and I normally parked. "Wyatt should be done with football by now. I can text him to pick one up for us."

"I never say no to pizza."

I grinned. "Neither do I."

This thing with us was good—damn good. If Londyn had moved to Summers, this might have become a real thing. She'd only been here for a couple of weeks and it was more real than anything I'd had in a decade.

I needed a woman like her, who loved pizza more than the number on her bathroom scale. A woman who spent time on my boat happy with long periods of time when not a word was spoken. A woman who preferred eating dinner on a rock to a fancy restaurant.

Londyn would be perfect if she weren't so hell-bent on leaving.

Then again, maybe the reason we clicked so well was because there was a time limit.

Leaving that thought untouched, I got out of the truck, rounding the back to open Londyn's door. Then I took her hand and walked her into the shop. I inserted my key into the lock, meeting no resistance as I turned.

Fuck. My stomach clenched. This door should have been locked, something Tony would have done before going home. I took a few steps back, glancing around the corner of the building to see if Tony's truck was still here. Maybe he'd parked alongside the tow rig today, but that space was empty.

"What?" Londyn asked.

"The door's unlocked." I went back to the handle, turning it slowly as I poked my head inside. "Hello?"

The shop was pitch black. My voice bounced off the walls but otherwise, the garage was silent. I flicked on a row of lights, stepping inside.

Behind me, Londyn put a hand on my back, the pressure gentle as she followed me down the hallway and into the main room. I flipped on a row of lights, scanning the place.

Nothing seemed out of the ordinary until Londyn gasped.

"Wha—" I followed her gaze to the Cadillac's tires.

They were slashed.

I rushed to the car, walking all around it as I inspected it from roof to wheel and bumper to fender. There wasn't a thing wrong with it except all four tires had been cut, the rubber dangling from the rims.

"Fuck." I raked a hand through my hair. I should have taken that key from Moira when I'd gone to her house. I'd been impatient to leave. I thought she'd done her worst and I could have Wyatt get it from her later. That mistake was on me.

"Was this—"

"Moira? Yeah," I clipped. "I'm calling the cops."

I dug my phone from my pocket, ready to dial the sheriff, but Londyn stopped me with a hand on my arm.

"What if it wasn't her?"

"Who else could it be?"

She frowned. "*My* ex."

"You think?"

"Well, the first time, I would have said no. But Thomas knows I'm here and he's been trying for months to get me to listen to him. What he wants more than anything is for me to come back to Boston."

"But wouldn't we have seen him around town? He doesn't strike me as the kind of guy who'd lurk in corners."

Thomas was an arrogant, rich asshole. He'd driven to Summers and found Londyn immediately. He was bold, not a coward who trashed a woman's car in secret.

"Maybe that investigator he hired did it for him? I don't know." Her eyes dropped to the tires and she pressed her fingertips to her temples. "I can't believe this."

"Me neither." I hung my head. "It's just tires."

"This is crazy. Totally insane. I feel . . . violated. This is my car. My beautiful car. It doesn't deserve this."

"I'm sorry. I'm so sorry." I pulled her into my side. "I can fix it. All I have to do is get the tires ordered. It's past time for a Friday, but I can place the order and they'll be here on Monday. You just might not be able to leave first thing in the morning."

"That's fine," she muttered, her eyes still locked on the gashes in the rubber. "If your ex is so desperate to get rid of me, why do this? I don't think it was her. If she had left them alone, I would have been gone already."

My stomach tightened at the idea of having lost her a week ago. I hated the shit with her car, but I'd gotten time with Londyn we otherwise would have missed.

But it had to be her. This was so damn familiar, it made me sick. When the fuck would Moira grow up?

"She's got to be worried that you might stay," I said. "This is her way of trying to run you out of town."

"Or it's not her." Londyn dug the phone from her purse, the one I'd given her. "This feels slimy and devious. A year ago, I wouldn't have said that was Thomas, but it turns out I didn't know my husband all that well. I'm going to make a call."

"Okay." I kissed her hair. "I'll leave you alone and go order your tires."

"Thanks." Her shoulders fell as she dialed the number.

I disappeared into the office, collapsing into my chair. "Fuck."

Why was this happening? I could hear Londyn talking, but I didn't need to know what her ex was going to say. He hadn't slashed her tires.

This had Moira written all over it.

Why couldn't she just let me move on? I didn't wish her to live a lonely life. She didn't date but I wouldn't stand in the way if she wanted to. I swiped up the handset of the phone on the desk and punched in her number.

She answered on the first ring. "Hey."

"Why'd you do it?"

"Hello to you too."

"She's leaving, Moira. She's not a threat. But this whole *if I can't have you, no one can* attitude is getting old. Leave her alone. Leave her car alone."

Silence. One moment later, I got the dial tone.

It wasn't the first time Moira had hung up on me and it wouldn't be the last. I set the handset in the cradle and sighed.

Londyn's voice drifted into the office from the shop, and though I knew I shouldn't listen in, I did anyway.

"I'm sorry, Thomas."

That caught my attention. Why was she apologizing? For calling? I sat motionless, my ears searching for more.

"Goodbye." Londyn let out a groan, then her footsteps shuffled toward the office.

"Not him?" I asked as she leaned against the doorframe.

"Nope. He's in Boston with Secretary . . . his girl-friend. Or mistress. Whatever she is. Her name is Raylene."

"He cheated on you?"

She nodded. "With the woman who sat across from my desk. Raylene was his *other* assistant."

That hadn't come up in all our conversations. If I hadn't asked her earlier this week about being a rebound, I might have doubted her motivation for being with me had I known Thomas was a cheat. But I believed Londyn.

Nothing about this felt shallow or distant. She was in this, all in this, just like me.

"Damn." Now I was really curious why she'd apologized to the asshole.

"She's pregnant."

"What?" My jaw fell open. So this guy had cheated on her and gotten her coworker pregnant? I should have hit him when I'd had the chance. "Wow."

"Pretty much." She closed her eyes. "Well, she *was* pregnant. She had a miscarriage. When I called, he was at the hospital with her."

"Shit." I leaned my elbows on my knees. "That's awful."

"I feel horrible. I don't like either of them, but I wouldn't wish that on anyone." She came into the office and sank into the guest chair. "I guess we know that Thomas didn't have anything to do with my tires. I doubt he would have lied to me, not today."

"I get why you called to ask, but Londyn, it's Moira. I called her when I got in here and she didn't even deny it."

"Maybe dinner with Wyatt isn't a good idea." She gave me a sad smile. "You eat with him tonight. Spend time with your son. Come over to the motel if you want later. And by Monday, Moira will have nothing to be worried about."

Yeah, she was leaving, but she wasn't gone yet.

"She doesn't get to win." I stood and waved her out of the office. I hadn't ordered her tires, but I'd call them in later. We were going to eat pizza with my son and hang out at my house. Her motel room was just another reminder that she was leaving, and I'd be damned if I spent another night there when I had a perfectly good bed at my own place. "Come on."

"Where are we going?" she asked as I turned off the light behind her. "Brooks, we don't need to make this a thing with your ex. She's crazy. You're pissed. I'm pissed. But they're only tires."

"Tires are expensive. What she did isn't okay." I took Londyn's hand, trapping it in my grip as we walked through the shop to the back door.

She tugged on my arm, slowing my pace. "Normally, I'd say go after her. But not today. I'm leaving Monday and I don't want this to be a thing. She gets away with it this time."

I frowned. "I'm calling the cops."

"And what will they do? Arrest her? Fine her? While we stand here for hours getting questioned for a report? I don't want to spend my last days in Summers with the cops."

I didn't either. But I was done with shit from Moira. She didn't get to act like a brat and cost me time and money. If she wouldn't listen to me, maybe the sheriff would have more influence.

"Let's call it a day." Londyn squeezed my hand.

No fucking way. "What kind of pizza do you like?"

"Uh . . . I'm not picky but—"

"Wyatt likes pepperoni, sausage, bacon and ham."

"That's a lot of meat."

"He's a growing boy." I looked down at her. "You good with that or do you need some veggies on there too?"

"I wouldn't say no to onion, green pepper and olives. But I don't need them if he's picky."

I was glad to see she was done objecting, not that I was taking no for an answer. "Wyatt will eat anything with cheese and meat on it."

I pushed through the door, holding it open for Londyn. Then I locked it up, not that it mattered now. Moira had done her damage.

The tires sucked. But I'd deal, like always. I'd make it right. And for tonight, I wasn't going to let it take away from my time with Londyn. She seemed to be letting it go too. Either she was the most easy-going woman in the world, or she was cherishing this time together too.

We climbed in my truck and I called Wyatt with instructions for pizza. He agreed to pick it up on his way home.

"Should we get something for dessert?" Londyn asked as we pulled away from the shop.

"I'll make brownies."

She raised an eyebrow. "You can make brownies? I feel like I've been cheated this past week."

I chuckled. "I'll make it up to you in my bedroom."

"Your bedroom? I'm spending the night?"

"Let's give the motel a rest. What do you say?"

"Is that appropriate if Wyatt is at home?"

I liked that she cared about my son. "He's sixteen. He knows what I've been doing every night this week."

"Me. You've been doing me."

"That's right." I grinned. "Every chance I get."

CHAPTER TWELVE

LONDYN

"Morning," I said as I came into the kitchen. Brooks stood by the stove, stirring scrambled eggs in a frying pan. The smell of fresh coffee and bacon drifted around the room, making my mouth water. As did the chef. He was dressed in olive cargo shorts and a black T-shirt, the logo on the front for the garage. His hair was still damp from his shower.

I had fully intended to go to the motel after pizza last night, but Brooks was stubborn and tricky. He hadn't asked me to stay, he'd just made it happen. He'd worn me out in his bed until I'd passed out, blissfully sated. I'd woken up alone in his massive bed this morning as the sun streamed through his bedroom windows.

Waking up by sunshine was now a must for all future days.

Brooks looked fresh and clean and delicious. I was in

yesterday's tank top and shorts, using my swimsuit as underwear.

I walked up behind him, rising on my toes for a kiss. "I'm going to get out of here before Wy—"

"Morning, Dad. Miss Londyn." Wyatt came into the kitchen wearing nearly the same thing as his father, except his Cohen's Garage T-shirt was gray and his shorts tan.

"Hey, kid. You hungry?" Brooks asked over his shoulder.

"Starving." Wyatt took a seat at the kitchen island, his eyes foggy with sleep. He blushed when he met my gaze, then dropped his eyes to the plate Brooks had set out already.

Oh, shit. Had he heard us last night? I looked up at Brooks, mortified that his son might have heard me moaning into a pillow, but he was no help. He shrugged.

"I'm gonna go," I mouthed.

"Coffee or orange juice?"

"Orange juice. But—"

"Wyatt, will you get Londyn a glass of orange juice? And pour one for me and you too, please."

"Sure, Dad." He yawned, sliding off his stool.

"Brooks, I'm a wreck. I'm wearing a swimsuit and yesterday's clothes," I whispered.

He leaned in close as Wyatt shuffled around the kitchen, getting our drinks. "You can change after breakfast."

"I can't stay and eat with you guys. It's bad enough I'm doing the walk of shame in front of your son."

"He's sixteen, not six. Besides, it's your turn. I've been doing the walk of shame past Meggie for a week."

"This is totally different."

A grin tugged at his lips. "Wyatt, do you care if Londyn is wearing the same clothes she was yesterday?"

"Brooks," I hissed, swatting him in the chest at the same time Wyatt said, "No."

"See?" Brooks smiled. "Go sit down. This is ready."

"Fine," I muttered, going to the island. I took the stool on the right, leaving the one between me and Wyatt for Brooks. He came over with the pan, plated our eggs and returned with a heaping plate of bacon. "That's a lot of pork."

Brooks nodded at Wyatt. "Remember what I told you yesterday? Growing boy."

"I don't think I'll ever forget seeing one person consume an entire extra-large pizza."

Wyatt stayed quiet—*was he sleepwalking?*—then piled a fistful of bacon strips on top of his eggs.

"Wyatt takes a while to wake up," Brooks said.

But he had no problem eating. The teenager dove into his plate with the same gusto as he had the pizza last night. By the time he'd shoveled half his eggs and two strips into his mouth, he seemed coherent. "What time are we leaving today, Dad?"

"I don't know," Brooks said, taking bacon for his own

plate and putting one piece on mine. "How long will it take you to get ready?"

When Wyatt didn't answer, I looked up to find Brooks had asked me the question. "Me? Get ready for what?"

"We're spending the day at my parents' place."

"No." The son was one thing, but his parents? Never happening.

"Why not? They're the best and it'll be fun. We're taking their boat out."

"Granddad's boat is twice as big as Dad's," Wyatt said with his head bent over his plate between inhaled bites.

"That's nice." I leaned forward to smile at Wyatt, then leaned back to frown at his father. "No."

"You should come." Wyatt crunched a bite of bacon.

"She's coming." Brooks pointed his fork at my plate. "Eat."

I rolled my eyes and focused on my meal. I'd eat and disappear before the Cohen men cornered me into attending a family event.

When my plate was clear, I took it to the sink, rinsing it before putting it in the dishwasher. Then I was gone, practically running through the kitchen for the hallway that led to the front door. "Bye, Wyatt!"

"Bye, Londyn," he called back.

I was three feet away from the door when a beefy arm wrapped around my waist and hauled me into an equally beefy chest. For a man this large, he sure could sneak up on a person. "Damn it."

"An hour," Brooks said into my ear.

"Brooks, I don't—"

"One hour."

I squirmed out of his hold to face him. "I don't belong at a Saturday family event. You guys go. Have fun. I'll see you tonight."

"It's a low-key thing. Come with us."

"Why? I'm a stranger. In two days, I'll be gone and a memory. Your parents will forget me before summer's over."

That earned me a scowl. "You won't be forgotten."

"Yes, I will."

"Not by me. And someday, I might want to talk about you. The only people who know you are Meggie and Wyatt. Love Meggie, but I don't see her much even though I live next door. And Wyatt will be gone to college before I blink. My parents, they rank right up there as my favorite people. So one day when I want to talk about the woman who came into my life and turned it upside down for a couple weeks, it sure would make that conversation easier if they knew what you looked like."

"Oh." How could I argue with that? I liked that he wanted to talk about me. I liked that he would remember me, even though I was sure his parents wouldn't.

I'd remember him too.

For the rest of my life.

"Okay." I nodded. "I'll go shower and be ready in an hour."

"Thank you." He took my face in his palms, bending as he pulled me up to his mouth. The kiss was soft but short. They were all too short, even the kisses that lasted all night. Brooks let me go and opened the door for me, sending me on my way.

The heat soaked into my skin as I crossed the lawn from his house to the motel. As I walked, I tallied up the days I'd been here in Summers.

Sixteen. In a way, they'd been the longest sixteen days of my life. Each had been so full and enjoyable. Two weeks with another person had never felt so important as the sixteen days I'd been in Summers with Brooks.

This weekend was the end. Monday, I'd wake up knowing I wouldn't see him again. Would I really be able to drive away? I'd left countless people behind in my life. My parents. My teachers. My friends.

I'd known, walking away from them, it was unlikely we'd meet again. But I'd gone with a sense of adventure fueling my footsteps. I'd gone with excitement and anticipation of what was out there in this great big world.

And I hadn't looked back.

When I left Monday, I'd look back. I'd wonder.

How was Brooks doing at the garage? How was Wyatt? After he went to college, would Brooks get lonely? When would he find someone new?

Those questions would haunt me, especially the last.

But I had to leave. I wasn't going to stick around a town for a man, not again. How many experiences had I sacrificed for Thomas? How many opportunities had I missed because I'd been stuck in Boston?

This time in Summers was temporary. It was a gift.

I wasn't even that upset about the Cadillac. Normally, I'd have flown off the handle at two vandalisms. Police would have been called. Heads would have rolled. And though a part of me did feel violated, that vulnerability was easily overshadowed by the thrill of being with Brooks.

I didn't like that my most prized possession had been tarnished, but it was just an object. I'd learned a long time ago that possessions weren't important. You could walk away from belongings, homes and people and survive.

Sometimes, you thrived.

The extra time with Brooks was worth the Cadillac's weight in gold.

The heaviest thing on my mind wasn't my tires, but that phone call to Thomas. My heart went out to him and Secretary—Raylene. Knowing she was in pain had made her human again.

Did Gemma know about the miscarriage? Should I call? No, not yet. There wasn't time today. When I talked to her, I wanted to tell her about Brooks. I'd call once I was back on the road. There was no doubt I'd need a friend my first night away from Summers.

I'd call to tell her about the man who had become one of my favorite people in only sixteen days.

My motel room was quiet—lonely—and I rushed

through my shower. My suit got a thorough rinse even though it would be wet when I put it on. But since it was the only one I had, I'd deal with a damp suit.

When I was ready, dressed in the one and only dress I had in my possession, a sleeveless dusty-blue shift with a tie around the waist, I packed up my purse with my swimsuit wrapped in a white motel towel.

"Sunglasses." I looked around the room, remembering they were somewhere in Brooks's truck. I opened the door to find Wyatt, his knuckles raised to knock. "Oh, hi."

"Hi." He nodded, a gesture that seemed more like a bow. Such gentlemen, these Cohen boys. "Dad sent me over to get you."

"He was afraid I'd change my mind, wasn't he? And he thought I'd have a harder time saying no to you."

Wyatt gave me a sheepish nod.

I laughed, stepping outside and pulling the door closed. "Is this weird? Sorry if it's weird."

"No, ma'am."

"Londyn."

"Yes, ma'am—Londyn." Wyatt's natural stride was double mine, but he slowed as we walked toward his home. Brooks did the same thing when we walked together.

Though father and son had similar features, it was the way they acted that made their resemblance so uncanny. They held their forks the same way. They ate their pizza the same way, chewing with the same circular motion.

They talked the same way. When Wyatt's voice got deeper, I suspected it would be nearly impossible to tell them apart on a phone call.

"So, you're uh . . . leaving?" Wyatt kept his hands in his pockets and his eyes on the grass as he attempted to make conversation.

"Yes, on Monday."

"Will you keep in touch with Dad?"

"Maybe." *Maybe not.* Quitting Brooks cold turkey would probably be best for us both. I didn't want to string this out until the phone calls spanned more time. Until one or both held some resentment that we'd drifted apart.

"You should," Wyatt said. "Dad doesn't have many close friends. Especially women. He's kind of wary about them."

Because his mom was crazy and the women in town were terrified Moira would hack out a kidney with a car key. Suffice it to say, I wasn't a fan of his mother.

"Oh really?" I feigned surprise.

"A lot of women in town only want Dad because of his money."

"Huh." Brooks had money?

I studied the house as we approached, not seeing anything that screamed big money. It was nice—classic and warm—but it didn't scream wealth. He had a boat. He had a nice truck. Maybe Brooks was rich for Summers's standards.

I gave myself a mental eye roll. Once, as a teenager, I

would have thought Brooks's house was a palace. Being married to Thomas had skewed my perspective too far. He had more money than I'd be able to spend in two lifetimes.

Brooks came out the front door, carrying a small blue cooler in one hand and my sunglasses in the other. "Here, honey."

"Thanks." I smiled. I always did when he called me honey.

His endearment came so naturally. He said it with such ease, I'd wondered at first if maybe he called all women honey. But as time went on, I realized it was mine. It was another gift.

I hadn't owned an endearment before. My parents hadn't bothered because they weren't endearing people. Thomas had called me Londyn and only Londyn. Even Karson had stuck to my name or Lonny, like Gemma still used.

Honey. I tucked the word into my pocket for later.

I glanced at Wyatt as I put my sunglasses on. He was trying to hide a smile.

"You can sit up front." He opened my door for me, then helped me inside. Then he climbed in the truck, sitting behind me as Brooks got behind the wheel.

Brooks asked Wyatt questions about football as we drove across town, taking inventory of the plays Wyatt needed to memorize before the weekend was over. As we neared the edge of town, the homes became larger and more spread apart. I wasn't sure how far we were going until Brooks eased off the gas to turn toward the lake. An iron gate greeted us at the end of a private drive.

He rolled down his window and punched a code into the keypad, then steered us on the tree-lined drive until a sprawling cream house came into view.

Ahh. Now I understood Wyatt's comment about money. Brooks Cohen, or rather his parents, must have it in spades. This was the nicest home I'd seen in Summers, and though it was tasteful for this town and not arrogant in size or style, it stood apart. It was probably six thousand square feet with a looped driveway, much like the one I'd left behind in Boston. A barn with a gable roof sat in the distance. Two dogs lazed beside a koi pond. And like Brooks's home, this home's windows were the focal point. They gleamed, reflecting the shine bouncing off the lake.

"Your dad is a doctor, right?" I asked.

"He is. Still works at the hospital because he says he's too young to retire. Mom stayed home and looked after me and my sister. You'll meet her today." He dropped his voice. "And a few others."

Behind me, Wyatt let out a snort.

I looked between him and Brooks. Both were avoiding eye contact and holding back grins. "Okay, what am I missing?"

They bolted from the truck before answering.

I shot Brooks a glare as he rounded the hood to open my door. When my foot hit the concrete, I opened my mouth to demand details about this *low-key thing*—and a crowd of people rushed out of the house.

Wyatt got swallowed up first. Then the swarm descended on us.

"Hi, Londyn." Brooks's mom enveloped me in a hug. "We're so glad you could come today."

"Thanks for having me . . ." I looked at Brooks in panic. What was her name? He hadn't told me their names.

"Ava," he mouthed.

"It's lovely to meet you, Ava."

"My, you are pretty." She winked at me, then pulled Brooks into a hug. "Hello, son."

"Hi, Mom." He tucked her into his side just as I was wrapped up again, this time by Brooks's father.

"Carter Cohen. Great to meet you." He slapped a hand to my back.

Whoa. He was as strong as Brooks. "You too."

He released me, grinning from ear to ear as the rest of the people around us started tossing out names I had no hope of remembering. I got lost in the handshakes and hugs.

I met Brooks's sister and her husband while their two small children chased around Wyatt's legs. There was an aunt and a great aunt. There were five or six uncles, or was one of them a cousin?

It took me the entire day to get it all straight, but by the time dinner was over and I was sitting on the back deck,

I'd finally put names and relations to each face. I'd even managed to figure out which twin uncle was Henry and which was Harry.

Brooks and I were sharing a lounge chair. When I'd moved to take my own, he'd hauled me down on his lap. His fingers idly caressed my bare knee.

"So?" Brooks raised an eyebrow as he spoke low so only I'd hear. "What'd I tell you?"

"It was fun." I smiled. "You have a wonderful family."

"Sure do."

He was fortunate. He *knew* he was blessed. These people were genuine and kind. They'd pulled me into their family today like I'd been here for years. Like I'd *be* here for years.

Brooks, Wyatt and I were the only three guests left at Carter and Ava's house. Everyone else had gone home about an hour after dinner, but we'd been in no rush to leave. I wasn't ready to end this day yet.

We'd spent most of the morning and afternoon on the lake, alternating groups on the boat to go skiing or surfing or tubing. Once the boat was docked, we'd played lawn games, holding competitions in bocce ball and cornhole. I'd laughed more today than I had all year. I'd also discovered I had a competitive streak when it came to lawn darts.

After games, we'd congregated on the sprawling deck, eating a feast that Ava had prepared, forgoing some of the outdoor fun. Brooks had promised me that feeding us was her kind of fun.

Ava was an authentic mother, nurturing and kind. Today was the first time I'd seen one in real life.

This entire experience was a first. This family laughed and teased one another. When they asked about each other's jobs or homes or cars, it was with genuine interest. They knew what was happening in each other's lives because they weren't only blood relatives, they were friends.

I hadn't had that since the junkyard.

Thomas was an only child and his parents lived in Boston for a third of the year, at most. I'd missed feeling like I belonged to more than just one person. That if I needed help, I'd have an entire posse at my back.

I wouldn't forget these people. I wouldn't forget this day.

Maybe this remarkable family wouldn't soon forget me either.

"I'm hungry," Wyatt announced from the seat beside us.

"Seriously?" I asked. "You just ate a full rack of ribs, two ears of corn and half a dozen rolls."

Yes, I was keeping track of Wyatt's food consumption. It was fascinating, seeing a boy with not an ounce of fat eat more than I did in a week.

He shrugged. "But I didn't get dessert."

"Pie." Brooks sat up, taking me with him as he stood from the chair. "Wyatt's hungry and I want pie."

"The diner?" Carter stood too, holding out a hand to help Ava from her seat.

"I hope they have a slice of pecan left," she said, smiling as she led the way into her house.

The kitchen was state of the art, but there were magnets on the fridge, holding up art made by Carter and Ava's grandchildren. Pictures adorned the walls instead of expensive paintings. The house had beautiful furniture, each piece top of the line, but comfortable. I wouldn't be afraid to sit on a couch and tuck my feet up.

It was a home and the heart of this family.

And I don't belong.

The realization slammed into me as I walked down the hallway and passed a collage of framed Christmas cards. An overpowering urge to get in my car and drive far away hit. This life wasn't mine. I'd pretended today, but this wasn't my family. It never would be.

It was time to go.

The urge to leave settled deep in my bones. I'd had the same feeling at sixteen years old. Again, at eighteen. Again, at twenty and twenty-one. And again, weeks ago, when I'd packed up and left Boston.

It was time to go.

I followed Brooks to his truck, hopping in and buckling my seat belt. Then I wrapped my arms around myself. Maybe if I squeezed hard enough, the feeling would go away. Though my mind knew it was time, my heart wasn't ready to leave, not yet.

One more day.

"You okay?" Brooks asked as he got in the truck. "Cold?"

"Just a little." I forced a smile. "Nothing some pie won't fix."

He turned the heat on for me, even though it was still sweltering outside.

I focused on the drive to town, on the homes and the trees and the quiet neighborhoods. The unsettling churn in my gut was still there when we reached the diner, but it wasn't nearly as potent. It faded to ignorable as we crammed into a booth.

"I'm squishing Londyn." Ava shifted in the seat. "Should we get a table instead?"

"No." I touched her arm before she could stand. "I don't mind the squish."

I was sandwiched between her and Brooks on one side of the booth while Carter and Wyatt were in the opposite. I didn't have a ton of room, but Brooks tossed his arm over the back of the seat so I could burrow into his side.

The waiter came over and we all placed our pie orders. He'd just collected our menus and disappeared to the kitchen when another figure appeared at the end of the table.

Brooks's spine went rigid as we all stared up at his red-faced ex-wife.

"Mom?" Wyatt's forehead furrowed. "What are you doing here?"

"You called the cops on me?" she hissed at Brooks.

Oh, shit. When? I thought he'd decided to leave it alone yesterday when we'd left the garage.

"I told you I would," he said. "You crossed the line."

"No, you did." Moira pointed at him. "I didn't do anything to her car."

"Mom." Wyatt stood, placing his hand on her arm.

She turned her eyes up to her son. They softened, pleading for him to believe her. "I didn't do anything to her car."

Uh . . . I didn't know Moira, but that sounded a lot like the truth.

Wyatt gave her a sad smile, then pulled her in for a hug.

She held him tight, then let him go and was out the door as quickly as she'd appeared.

"What was that about?" Carter asked Brooks as Wyatt took his seat.

"Someone's been vandalizing Londyn's car," Brooks answered. "Keyed it last week. Poured paint all over it. Yesterday, we found all four tires slashed."

Ava sucked in a sharp breath, covering my hand with hers.

Carter hung his head. "When's that girl gonna learn?"

"It's okay," I told the table, my eyes aimed at Wyatt, whose shoulders were hunched forward. "It's just a car and I'm only passing through. On Monday, this won't be a problem."

Brooks's arm tightened around my shoulder.

"Are you sure it's Mom?" Wyatt asked his dad.

"I don't know, kid. I wish I could say it wasn't, but your mom's done stuff like this before."

"I know she flies off the handle, but she's been different lately. Happier, I guess. She's been seeing this guy and he's . . . nice."

"She has?" Brooks leaned forward. "Who?"

It wasn't a jealous question, more concern that another man was hanging out with his kid and he was just learning about it.

"A guy from Oak Hill. They mostly go out when I'm with you, but I've met him a couple of times. He seems like a good guy. He mellows Mom."

"Hmm." Brooks's forehead furrowed.

"Did you consider it might not be her?" Ava asked. "I know you two have had a rocky relationship, but Brooks, I know that girl. And while I wouldn't put it past Moira to do something foolish in the heat of the moment, that didn't sound like a lie."

"No, it didn't." Brooks ran a hand over his face. "Damn it. I'll call her tonight," he promised Wyatt. "I'll make it right."

Wyatt sighed, picking up his fork. "Thanks, Dad."

"So . . ." Carter met Brooks's gaze, then they both turned to me. "If it wasn't Moira, who is vandalizing your car?"

CHAPTER THIRTEEN

LONDYN

"What's all this?" I asked Brooks. His kitchen island was piled with plastic food containers, each with the lid securely shut.

"A picnic."

"Really?" I smiled. I'd never gone on a picnic before, not a proper one. The days at the junkyard when we'd eat on our laps in Gemma's tent didn't count.

Brooks walked to the large pantry off the kitchen and came back with a basket. It was a rich, tawny cedar with a red, white and blue plaid lining. The lids flipped up from the middle, one side at a time.

He owned an actual picnic basket. Why did that make me want to cry?

I looked away, blinking and swallowing away the emotion. I'd been on the verge of tears for hours.

Tomorrow was Monday and I'd been letting my upcoming departure stain our day.

Brooks and I had spent the day together doing normal things any person did on a Sunday to prepare for a workweek.

We'd gone to the grocery store. I'd had to hide my quivering chin in the checkout line for no good reason other than we'd piled our stuff together on the conveyor belt. My bottle of body wash and toothpaste had been sandwiched between a bag of baby carrots and jug of cranberry juice. The cashier had rung it all up and Brooks had helped pack everything into his reusable grocery bags. I'd stood by, not listening as he'd chatted with her because I'd been trying to figure out why I'd been so close to crying. Was it the baby carrots or the blue grocery bags?

I'd analyze it later when I was on the road.

Just like I'd analyze why I'd gotten choked up in the laundry room earlier. I'd washed all of my clothes in Brooks's machine today, preparing to pack them into my suitcases. When I'd poured the detergent into the machine, the scent of his clothing and bedsheets had brought out a miserable sting in my nose. One tear had actually escaped before I'd shut the others down.

It was definitely time to go.

Hopefully tomorrow my car would be ready too, and I could escape Summers before it became another cage.

"How did your call with Moira go?" I asked Brooks.

A crease formed between his eyebrows. "As good as

expected. She's pissed and has a right to be pissed. But she won't stay mad at me forever."

"That's good." I looked around the kitchen as he finished up. The smell of bacon hung in the air from this morning's breakfast. "Where's Wyatt?"

"He went to Moira's."

"Oh." A sting laced my heart. Was he coming back? Or had I missed my chance to say goodbye? While Brooks and I had run errands today, Wyatt had been at home. He'd been on the couch in the living room, his eyes glued to his phone. He'd been in the exact same spot when we'd returned.

Then I'd left for thirty minutes to take my clean clothes to the motel. I hadn't noticed his truck was gone when I'd walked back. "I guess . . . will you tell him goodbye for me?"

Brooks abandoned the basket and came around the island, wrapping me in his arms. "He'll be back in the morning before football practice. He just went to stay at Moira's so we could have some privacy."

"Oh, good." I relaxed into his arms.

"Come on." He kissed me on my hair and let me go to collect the picnic basket.

As I followed Brooks through the house, my eyes zoomed around, soaking in a final farewell. There were two bedrooms on the main floor. One was Wyatt's and the other Brooks had turned into an office, while the master and another bedroom were upstairs.

193

It wasn't the pieces or the layout of this house I'd remember. It was the sense of peace and comfort. Nothing matched and there was no theme. The artwork was random, some photographs and some prints scattered throughout. The furniture was leather in varying shades.

Nothing here had been styled or decorated. When I thought of the interior designer Thomas had hired to *incorporate my tastes* into his home, I let loose a wicked smile. She'd hate that Brooks's toss pillows were actually used to support heads while watching football games on Sundays. She'd hate that the coffee table didn't have a single coaster.

Brooks opened the back door that led to the outside deck. The instant he passed the table covered with a white umbrella, I knew exactly where we were headed.

"The rock?"

He grinned down at me as we crossed the grass, both of us in bare feet. "Thought it would be appropriate for our last dinner. Have it where we had our first."

"That sounds wonderful."

I'd been waiting all week for Brooks to ask me to stay again. But he hadn't, not once, since I'd turned him down, probably because we both knew the answer wouldn't change. My tires would show up at the garage tomorrow. He'd work on them as soon as they arrived, then I'd be on the road. My goal was to make it to Kentucky and stay in Lexington or Louisville tomorrow night.

For the foreseeable future, I'd stick to the interstate.

No off-road detour would ever compare to this stop in Summers. California was waiting and I was anxious to see what—and who—I'd find.

"I've been thinking about something," I said as we reached the rock and situated ourselves in our normal spots. We'd gotten lucky for the night and the heat had given us a break. The humidity was thick but it was bearable for dinner.

"What's that?" Brooks set the basket aside, giving me his full attention.

"I'm going to Temecula. I figure that's the best place to start my search for Karson."

"Agreed."

"Maybe . . ." I mustered up the courage to voice a thought that had been plaguing me since leaving his parents' house yesterday. "Maybe I should find out what happened to my parents."

He blinked. Twice. "Why?"

"I've thought more about them these past couple of weeks than I have in years. And being around your parents made me wonder about my own. Maybe it's a crazy idea and bound to be a disaster."

"I'd say it's normal for a child to want to know about their parents."

"They never tried to find me." My gaze drifted across the water. "If they did, they didn't try hard, but I'm still curious. I left them as an angry, neglected teenager. Maybe seeing them as an adult will give me some closure."

What if they'd turned their lives around? What if they hadn't? I wasn't sure how I'd feel if I found them in the same dirty trailer—or the cemetery. Had I become an orphan while traveling the country? Did I want to know badly enough? Did I have the courage to show up at my former home and knock on the door alone?

"What would you do?" I asked.

"The truth?" He raised an eyebrow and I nodded. "Fuck 'em. They don't deserve you."

That's what Gemma always said. None of our parents had deserved us as kids.

"You're probably right. I'll think on it longer." Maybe by the time I hit Arizona, I'd have my feelings about them in order. "Let's eat."

"This isn't fancy." Brooks opened up the basket and took out a green container for me, then another for himself.

"I don't need fancy." My favorite sandwich was still peanut butter and grape jelly. I'd eaten countless numbers of them. In Boston, I'd sneak into the kitchen on late nights when I couldn't sleep and make one for myself. The chef kept the supplies in the pantry for me, despite Thomas's insistence that we could afford *decent* sandwich ingredients.

My heart craved simplicity, like a picnic on a rock.

I popped the top off the plastic container and the smell of bacon and tomato and bread wafted into the air. I inhaled the scent of my second-favorite sandwich. "So that's why you hid some bacon from Wyatt this morning."

Brooks chuckled. "I knew it would be safe in the vegetable drawer, tucked under the lettuce."

He finished taking out the containers from the basket. When it was all laid out, he'd packed us a feast, including some of the potato salad Ava had made yesterday. Brooks must have noticed I'd gone back for seconds. We ate without fanfare, enjoying the food and a Sunday evening with the lake glittering under the descending sun.

We didn't fill the hours on the rock with conversation or questions—there wasn't much more to say. The light faded and my eyelids drooped, but I couldn't find the strength to leave. Brooks didn't seem to want to leave our spot either. *Our spot.* God, I hoped he never let another woman kiss him on this rock.

We sat there until the blue sky darkened and the white crescent moon peeked out from behind the trees on the horizon.

"There's a star." He pointed above us. "Make a wish."

I closed my eyes, sending my wish to the galaxy, knowing this one wouldn't come true. "Done."

"Did you make it a good one?"

I found his hand between us. "I wished you would come with me. I can tell you that because I know it won't come true. But I wished it anyway."

His other hand came to his heart, his eyes clouded

with sadness. "In a different life, I'd drive around the world with you in that Cadillac."

But he had a son. He had a business and a life in Summers. And the reality was, I needed to take this trip alone. The only person who could guide *me* back to *me* was myself.

"This has been the best week of my life," I whispered. "Thank you. I'll never forget you."

"Same, honey." He cupped my cheek. "Same."

A tear dripped free and he caught it with his thumb. I sucked in a deep breath and began putting the containers into the basket, busying my hands and mind before I gave into the damn cry that wouldn't stay buried.

I was sniffling, snapping the lid on a container, when Brooks took it from my hands and dropped it in the basket. Then he took my face in his hands and brought his lips to mine, kissing away the sadness.

My arms snaked around his shoulders as his arms banded around my back, pulling me into his chest as we clutched one another.

The picnic basket was forgotten on the rock as Brooks and I fumbled our way to his house. We left a trail of clothes on the way to his room upstairs, breaking the kiss only to shed our shirts. When we reached his bed, my heart was racing and my body aching.

Brooks laid me down, covering me with his weight. His arms bracketed my face and his hips rested against my own. His cock was hard and thick between us as it nestled against my core.

We stilled. Our eyes locked. Our breaths mixed. His heartbeat drummed in the same thundering rhythm as my own.

"Don't forget me," I whispered. I'd been forgotten by too many people. I couldn't bear the idea of Brooks forgetting me too.

"I'll remember you until the end, Londyn." Brooks ran his knuckles along my cheek, leaving a trail of sparks on my skin. "Until the end."

I rose up and fused our mouths, giving him everything I had and trusting him with all my broken pieces.

Maybe he would forget me. Maybe time would dull his memories or disease would steal them away. But I hoped this kiss would remain.

I was falling for Brooks. I poured it into the kiss. If we had a month more or a year, he'd own my heart.

Brooks, this home and his family were enticing. What if I stayed? I'd have a home, a conventional, warm home, for the first time.

Not even Thomas had given me a home. We'd been two single pieces paired together for a while, but it hadn't made either of us whole. Brooks had the entire package. He was the corner to a thousand-piece jigsaw puzzle that created one stunning picture.

Staying was enticing. But the nagging feeling in my gut wouldn't go away, no matter how many times I kissed

Brooks. No matter how many times I closed my eyes and pictured myself living here.

The puzzle was built. There weren't any spaces for me to fill.

So I kept my eyes closed and savored the feel of his hands roaming across my skin, pretending this wasn't the last night. I pretended this was every night.

His kiss drifted down my neck and to the swell of my breast. Brooks tickled a nipple with his stubble before covering it with his mouth, rolling it over his tongue until he moved to do the same with the other.

My fingers wove through the golden strands of his hair, pulling him up to my lips once more. I let go with one hand and stretched for the end table drawer where he kept his stash of condoms.

He grinned when I handed it to him. "In a rush?"

"For you? Always." I smiled, waiting as he covered and positioned himself at my entrance. With a swift thrust, he stole my breath, filling me completely.

"So good," he groaned.

I nodded, tipping my hips to send him deeper. *So good.*

Brooks was the best lover of my life. He took control when we were together. His gaze raked over my body, appreciating every inch and banishing all insecurities. The man had a direct line to my brain. If I wasn't feeling something or he thought he could take me higher, he'd change direction, because it wasn't about him when we were together. It wasn't about me either.

It was about us.

He rocked us together, slowly at first until the pounding of our hearts matched the rhythm of his hips. The orgasm that built seemed to shroud us both, taking us racing toward the peak at equal speeds, until we came together, sweaty and breathless.

He left me for only a minute to take care of the condom, then he wrapped me in his arms and held me tight as we drifted off to sleep.

We woke twice more in the night, not wanting sleep to keep us apart, until morning finally forced us into the new day.

The dreaded Monday had dawned.

"What time should I come to the garage?"

Brooks stood in the bathroom, drying his wet hair with a towel. We'd showered together. I sat on his bed, wrapped in a fluffy gray towel.

He swallowed hard. "How about I drive the car to you? Then you don't need to worry about your suitcases."

"Okay."

I stayed on the bed—even as my hair grew cold on my bare skin—to listen as Brooks shaved his face and brushed his teeth. The weight of the day sank in and made my limbs nearly as heavy as my heart.

Don't let this be awkward. I closed my eyes, sending up a wish to the unseen stars. Brooks had been the best, most unexpected person to cross my path. We needed to end on a happy note—a kiss and a smile.

Brooks kissed me on the forehead as he walked to his closet.

Did he even realize how much he'd given me in our short time together? He'd shown me that leaving Boston had been the right decision. He'd shown me that there were kind, generous and loving men in the world.

Had I left him with anything good? Or after today, would I just be the woman who'd left?

Please, don't resent me.

I studied him as he dressed. When I pictured him in years to come, it would be in this room and in this moment.

He was barefoot in a pair of unbuttoned and faded jeans. His chest was bare and droplets of water clung to his shoulders. And his eyes were as blue as the sky on a West Virginia summer morning.

"Wyatt's coming over?" I asked.

He nodded as he tugged a green T-shirt off its hanger. He pulled it over his head just as the front door slammed downstairs. "Sounds like he's here."

"I'll get dressed and come down to say goodbye." I took a deep breath and stood from the bed.

Brooks nodded. "What would you like for breakfast?"

I gave him a sad smile. "I think I'll get a pastry from the motel today. You and Wyatt should get back to your normal routine anyway."

"Oh." His jaw tensed. "All right."

This wasn't all right but I feared no matter what I said, nothing would fix it. The awkwardness was coming.

I tied up my wet hair and rushed to pull on my clothes. Brooks was the one to sit on the bed now, watching as I scurried around his room.

"See you at four?"

He nodded, his eyes aimed at the floor.

I forced my feet through the bedroom door. I held my neck stiff, not letting myself twist and look back.

Wyatt was in the living room, standing beside the couch with his phone in his hands and his thumbs flying. I walked into his space and wrapped him up, trapping his arms at his sides. "Take care of him."

His stiff frame relaxed. "I will."

"It was nice meeting you." I let him go, unable to meet his eyes. Then I was out the door, jogging to the motel.

When I was locked inside my room, I leaned against the door, taking a moment for my heart to settle. I swiped away one tear and gritted my teeth to stop the others.

One goodbye down.

One more to go.

CHAPTER FOURTEEN

LONDYN

"Thanks for everything, Meggie." I tucked my credit card into my wallet, then stowed it in my purse.

"You're welcome." She leaned her elbows on the counter. "He didn't talk you into staying, huh?"

"No." I gave her a sad smile. "Have a great summer."

"You too." She sighed, then waved as I wheeled my suitcases to the door.

It was hot outside and I'd much rather wait in the air conditioning for Brooks to show with my car, but Meggie was itching for some gossip. I didn't have it in me to deflect her questions about my relationship with Brooks, not when all my energy was being used to fight the anxiety of the upcoming goodbye.

I pulled my luggage down the sidewalk to the corner of the motel, leaving it standing on the concrete while I took one last look at Brooks's house.

When I'd run away from home, I hadn't looked back at the trailer where I'd grown up. No matter how many years went by, that pile of filth was burned into my brain. The details lingered with perfect clarity.

My parents had been passed out in their bedroom that day, the same place they'd been for the three days prior. They did that, holed themselves up as they rode out their high. I used to peek in on them occasionally. Sometimes, I'd stand at the door and listen for any sound. The doors were so thin, if I listened close enough, I could hear them breathe.

It had taken me months to work up the courage to run. For nearly a year, I'd had a backpack stuffed with clothes and canned food. The final straw had been on the third day of a drug-induced disappearance. Mom and Dad had stayed quiet, too quiet, in their end of the trailer. No sound had even come from the TV. I'd gone to see if they were alive. When I'd cracked the door, Dad had been sitting up in bed, a rubber band tied tight around his bicep and a syringe poised at a vein. Mom had been asleep or passed out on her stomach at his side. Her nightstand had been crowded with half-empty bottles of brown liquor.

Dad's eyes had been glassy when they'd met mine. He'd stared at me for a long minute, tilting his head to the side. Was it regret I'd seen in his gaze that day? Or confusion? I'd never know. For a moment, I'd thought maybe he'd put the needle down. Instead, he'd muttered, "Shut the door, Londyn."

I'd shut the door. Then I'd gone to my room and collected my backpack.

Running had seemed like the best choice. No home at all was better than waiting around in a dirty trailer to open that door again, only to find the pair of them dead.

When would the image of that place fade? If I stared at Brooks's house long enough, would it become permanently ingrained too?

His home was so clean. The white siding was pristine. There was no cracking paint or water stains. The windows gleamed in the sunlight, and at the right angle, it was almost as if the glass didn't exist.

I squeezed my eyes shut, picturing the house in my head. When I opened them, a car coming down the street caught my eye.

My car.

Brooks rode handsomely behind the wheel. He was not going to make this easy on me, was he? The top was down and his eyes were covered with a pair of sunglasses. He drove with one hand while the other raked the hair away that had blown onto his forehead.

I didn't need to close my eyes to commit that image to memory for good.

Brooks pulled up to the curb and shut off the rumbling engine. "Well, it's about two weeks too late, but I can finally give you back your car."

I smiled, walking over to the Cadillac. I dropped my

purse in the passenger seat just as Brooks popped the trunk. I turned for my suitcases, but he stopped me.

"I'll get them." He swung those long legs out of the car, got out and loaded up my bags. Then he met me on the sidewalk beside the Cadillac. No one would have ever known it had been scraped on a guardrail, then gouged with a key. "Anything else?"

"No, that's it." I walked up close, placing my palm on his heart to feel the heat of him against my skin one last time. "Thank you."

"My pleasure." He shifted his sunglasses into his hair. "Promise me something."

"Okay." I nodded, tense as I waited for his demand. Would he ask me to stay? Or would he ask me to come back? If he asked me to return to Summers, I wouldn't be able to say no.

"Promise me if you ever need anything—a friend, a place to crash for a week, a piece of pie—you'll use that phone and call me."

I smiled, releasing the breath I'd been holding. "Promise."

My hand fell from his heart. My forehead took its place as I snaked my arms around his waist.

He wrapped me up tight, whispering into my hair. "Goodbye, Londyn McCormack."

I squeezed my eyes shut. "Goodbye, Brooks Cohen."

His hands came to my face, lifting my cheek off his

chest to brush his lips against mine. He broke the kiss too soon, and I took a step back.

I opened my mouth, but there was nothing more to say, so I walked around the hood of the car and settled into the driver's seat. I moved it up from where Brooks had adjusted it for his long legs. I shifted the mirrors. Then I gripped the steering wheel.

"All good?" Brooks leaned his elbows on the passenger door.

I nodded. "All good."

Except wasn't it supposed to feel like home? When I'd climbed behind the wheel in Boston, I'd been hit with such a sense of . . . rightness. That feeling was missing today. Maybe after a few miles I'd feel more comfortable in the seat.

A pained look crossed Brooks's gaze before he covered it with an easy, lopsided grin. He stood, tapped the side of the car with his knuckles and stepped back.

I twisted the key, igniting the engine to life. Then I gave him one last look before shifting the car into drive and easing away from the curb.

He lifted a hand to wave. I saw it from the corner of my eye but refused to turn. My eyes stayed fixed on the road ahead.

I made it twenty feet before my resolve shattered and I cast my gaze to the rearview mirror.

There he was, tall and strong, standing where the car had been with his hand held in the air.

"Damn it." Tears flooded my eyes but I kept my foot on the gas pedal. I only glanced at the road to make sure I wouldn't crash into the motel. Otherwise, my eyes were in the mirror.

Brooks stayed there, in that spot with his arm held high, until I rounded a bend in the highway and he was gone.

"Shit." I swiped at the tears as they dripped down my face. I sucked in a few deep breaths, trying to get my heart to sink down from my throat.

This would get easier, right? Maybe not today, maybe not tomorrow, but by the time I made it to California, I wouldn't feel so heartbroken.

I blew out a breath, rubbed the sting from my nose, then reached for the sunglasses I'd tucked into my purse. With them hiding my watery eyes, I focused on the road ahead.

Summers disappeared behind me quickly, but the first five miles past town were excruciating. So were the five after that.

It should feel better, shouldn't it? This is what I'd wanted, right? I was free to follow my own impulses. I wasn't trapped in the idea of someone else's conventional life.

I hauled my purse onto my lap, driving with one hand as I dug for the phone in the bottom. I pulled it out, needing to talk to someone who might understand why I was doing this.

"Hello?" Gemma answered my call on the second ring.

"Hey."

"Londyn? Where have you been? You promised you'd call." She sighed. "Are you okay?"

"I'm okay." A total fucking lie.

"Liar."

I huffed. "I'm not okay."

"Is this about . . ."

"No, this isn't about Thomas." I blew out a long breath, so long, she thought she'd lost me.

"Londyn?"

"I'm here." I looked in my rearview mirror, hoping to see Brooks and knowing I wouldn't. "I think I fell in love with someone."

"Already?" She laughed. "That doesn't sound like a problem to me."

"I just left him."

"Ah." The line went quiet.

"What do you mean, *ah*?"

"Nothing."

"Gem. Tell me."

She sighed. "It's just . . . this is what you do, Lonny. You get scared and run."

"What?" I switched my grip on the wheel so I could put the phone to the other ear. Clearly, I wasn't hearing her correctly. "I didn't run away from Boston because I was scared."

"Are you sure about that?"

Ouch. Okay, maybe calling my friend wasn't the right decision today. Gemma and I were always brutally honest with one another, but I wasn't emotionally stable enough for brutal today. Maybe I should have delayed this call a week or two.

"I left Boston to start over," I said. "It's time to simplify my life. I don't have this overwhelming desire to prove myself, Gem. I'm not like you. I don't need the money and the status."

"I don't need—ugh." She paused. "This isn't about me, and I don't want to fight."

I unclenched my jaw. "Me neither."

"I'm trying to help. You sound miserable. If you truly love this guy, whoever he is, then why are you leaving?"

"I don't know," I confessed.

"Are you afraid you'll find something real there?"

"Maybe I'm afraid I won't."

"Oh, Londyn." There was a smile in her voice. "It sounds like you already have. So why are you leaving?"

"I need to give this car to Karson. I need to see that he's okay."

"Do you have to do it today? Or tomorrow? Why not stay with this guy for a little while longer?"

"Brooks. His name is Brooks."

"Why not stay with Brooks?"

"Because." My heart hurt. The fears were working

themselves free, the feelings I'd buried for so, so long.

"Because what if he leaves me before I can leave him?"

That was the reason I ran, wasn't it? To get away from the big hurt. Maybe the reason I'd been able to stay with Thomas all these years was because I hadn't expected the end to hurt. It hadn't much.

Maybe the reason I'd felt trapped in Boston wasn't because I'd stayed in one place, but because that *one* place hadn't been the *right* place.

That goddamn Pottery Barn picnic basket flashed in my mind. Another woman didn't get to use that basket. It was mine.

So was Brooks.

"Turn the car around, Londyn," she said. "I'd give it all up—the company, the money, the power—to just feel *something.*"

Feelings for other people wasn't my problem. Sure, I ran from those feelings, but they were there, right on the surface. Not Gemma. As far as I knew, she'd never been in love.

"Don't waste it," she whispered.

I was throwing it away. I was driving away from a man who just might turn out to be the love of my life. I was driving away from a home.

"I kept having this feeling when I was walking around Summers—that's the town where I was. I felt . . . settled. Like things were calm in my soul. Do you think that's what it feels like to be home?"

"I don't know. I don't know if I've ever felt at home. But if I had to guess, I'd say yes."

Yes. Summers was home.

Brooks was home.

"I need to go."

Gemma laughed. "Is this a real number now? Can I call you?"

"Yeah." I smiled. "This is my number."

"Bye."

"Wait," I called before she could hang up. "Thanks."

"I miss you. Maybe I'll come visit you in—where are you?"

"West Virginia."

"West Virginia," she repeated. "Call me later."

"I will." I tossed the phone aside, sitting straighter in my seat. With both hands on the wheel, I eased off the gas pedal, searching the road ahead for a place to turn around. Of course, when I needed to flip a U-turn, there was nothing but a steep ditch and trees lining the road.

My eyes were on the shoulder when the car lurched. I gasped, snapping my gaze to the road. What the hell? Had I hit something?

I looked in the rearview mirror, jerking when my eyes landed on a large truck riding my bumper.

While I'd been on the phone with Gemma, I hadn't noticed it creep up on me.

"What the hell?" I muttered to the mirror, alternating my eyes on the road and the truck behind me.

Had he bumped me? Why would he hit my car? I was going ten miles an hour under the speed limit. Ten. Was contact necessary? Why not just pass me and be done with it?

I lifted my arm, waving him around, but as I watched through the mirror, the grill of the truck inched closer. My arms tensed and my grip on the wheel hardened. I braced for another bump.

It was no bump.

"Ah!" I screamed as he rammed me. The Cadillac lurched again, twice as hard as the first time.

The wheels veered on their own, from one edge of the lane to the other.

"Leave me alone!" I screamed.

He hit me again.

The Cadillac's tires screeched on the road, swerving from one white line to the next. Had there been an oncoming car, I would have crashed head-on.

I touched the brake.

The second I did, the truck's engine revved and he sped into the opposite lane.

I held my breath, thinking he'd race past me and probably give me the finger. Instead, he hovered in my blind spot.

"What?!" I glanced over my shoulder. I waved him around once more. The moment I lifted my hand off the wheel, he zoomed forward until he was right next to me. Still he didn't pass. He stayed in that lane, his passenger door so close I could have reached up and touched the handle.

The truck was too tall for me to see the driver this close. I pressed the brake to slow. The truck stayed in place, hovering at my same speed. My eyes scanned the edges of the road, hoping for a place where I could turn off and get away from this crazy asshole. There was nothing.

An oncoming car appeared.

"You crazy son of a bitch." I slowed more. The oncoming car's horn filled the air. "Go around!"

The truck didn't move.

Was this some kind of sick West Virginia version of chicken?

I slammed on the brake, my tires squealing on the blacktop, just as the truck sped up and swerved into my lane. I shimmied between the center lane and the ditch, the car heavy and sluggish to respond.

The oncoming car's horn blared as it flew past and I yanked the wheel to the safe side.

The correction was too much. Instead of staying between the lines, my front forward tire sank into the soft shoulder. When the front corner of the Cadillac dipped, I knew there was no saving me from a wreck.

The Cadillac dove off the side of the road. The vehicle rattled and bounced as it came to a punishing stop. My side of the car was tipped up at least three feet above the passenger side.

"Oh my God." I shook as I looked around, my entire

body trembling. The truck was gone. From the ditch, I couldn't see it race away, but the engine's roar faded in the distance.

I pushed the hair away from my face, taking stock of my body. I wasn't hurt, or if I was, I couldn't feel it yet. My fingers barely had the strength to turn the key and shut off the engine. I fumbled with the seat belt.

My purse was on the floor on the other side. I shoved myself out of the driver's seat, the angle requiring me to stand on the passenger-side door to keep my balance. Clutching the handle of my purse, I crawled out of the car into the ditch and took stock of the situation.

"No." My heart broke. My poor car. It was so much worse than it had looked from the seat. The front corner was crumpled. The whole thing was propped sideways against the ditch. The driver's-side tires were still digging into the loose asphalt of the road. Had the ditch been any steeper or the car's center any higher, I would have rolled.

My head spun and my hands shook. I fisted them, forcing the fear away for a moment to deal with this. I fought the urge to cry, focusing on the anger instead. "That fucking asshole!"

I climbed my way up the ditch on my hands and knees, wiping the dirt from my palms as I stood on the side of the road. I looked both ways.

I was alone.

But unlike my first flat tire, I wasn't helpless. I took the phone from my purse and called the one and only number saved in the contacts.

"Londyn?" Brooks answered. "You okay?"

"No." My voice shook. "I need you to come and get me."

"Where are you?" The sound of his boots echoed in the distance. "What the hell's going on? I'm worried."

"Don't worry." I blew out a breath and collected myself. "Just head out of town on the highway and you'll see me. And Brooks?"

"Yeah?"

I looked at my car. "Bring the tow truck."

CHAPTER FIFTEEN

BROOKS

"Are you okay?" Londyn asked, leaning into my side.

"Me?" I gaped at her. "Someone tried to run you off the fucking road. Are *you* okay?"

"I'm fine." She blew out a long breath, resting her cheek against my arm. "I won't be later, but at the moment, I'm okay and that's all that matters."

I clutched her hand, holding it tight like I had over the past hour. She was keeping it together at the moment, a credit to her incredible strength. But every five or ten minutes, a tremor would run through her body. Her grip on my fingers would tighten. If and when she fell apart later, it would be in the safety of my arms.

Whoever had done this to her would pay dearly.

We were standing on the side of the highway, waiting for the sheriff's deputy on the scene to finish taking photos of her car. He'd already taken her statement.

I'd listened with silent fury as Londyn had recapped the details of the accident. I should have thrown her keys in the damn lake and refused to let her leave town.

It seemed like days since she'd left me standing on the sidewalk outside the motel, not hours. For a moment, when I'd caught her looking at me in the rearview mirror, I'd thought maybe she'd turn back.

Maybe she'd prove us both wrong—maybe she'd make my life—and stay.

But she'd kept on driving. When her car had disappeared around a bend in the highway, it had been over. I sure hadn't expected her name to flash on my phone's screen so soon after she'd left—if ever.

The fear in her voice had had me racing through town in the tow truck. I'd been a goddamn scared mess when I'd shown up to find her car toppled sideways in the ditch. I'd pulled her in for a hug and hadn't let go, even when the cop had shown up. But the time to worry had passed and now I was fucking pissed.

This was attempted murder in my book and that meant years in prison. It didn't seem like enough.

"Brooks." The deputy waved me over. I refused to let go of Londyn's hand, so together, we met him by the hood of his cruiser, the lights still flashing on top. "I'm done here. You can load it up and take it back to town."

"Can I get going on repairs? Or do we need to leave it as is?"

"Hold for now. Let me confirm we don't need anything else for the investigation."

"There's no hurry," Londyn said. "Thanks for your help."

"Ma'am." He tipped his hat, then walked to his car, his notepad in hand. He stayed parked, slowing traffic, until I had the Cadillac winched out of the ditch and loaded on the flatbed.

It took me over an hour and I hated leaving Londyn alone in the truck, but I didn't want her standing on the road. Finally, as the afternoon faded to evening, I waved goodbye to the deputy and drove us down the road to Summers.

The time outside hadn't cooled my anger in the slightest. While I snarled over the steering wheel, Londyn kept her eerie calm in the passenger seat.

"I'm going to drop you off, then take the Cadillac to the shop."

"Okay." She sagged against the door. "Feels like we've been here before."

"Yeah." I barked a dry laugh as the motel came into view.

Londyn could sit at the motel with Meggie for an hour while I dropped off her car. There was no way in hell I was leaving her anywhere alone until we found the sick bastard who could have killed her today.

"I'm going to leave you with Meggie while I take the car to the shop. You can get settled at the motel. She'll be glad to have you back." We'd all be glad to have her back in Summers.

"The motel?" She sat up straight, then slapped a hand over her forehead. "Oh. Oh my God. I'm an idiot."

"Huh?"

"Nothing." She turned to the window. "Never mind."

I wasn't in the mood for never minds. "What did you mean, you're an idiot?"

"It's nothing." She waved it off.

"Londyn." My jaw clenched tight. "I'm hanging on by a thread here. Talk to me."

She hesitated, then looked my way. "You asked me to stay."

"And you said no." I remembered that word quite clearly from our conversation.

"You didn't ask again, and I thought you were just being understanding. I'm an idiot because I didn't even consider you might want me to go. That you were just in this for the short-term." Her voice cracked and she dropped her gaze to her lap.

"What the fuck are you talking about? How hard did you hit your head?" I studied her face. It was too pale. "I'm taking you to the hospital."

How could she think I didn't want her to stay? Watching her drive away had been ten times harder than I'd expected.

"I don't need to go to the hospital."

"If you think I *wanted* you to leave, then you're not thinking straight."

"You want me to stay?"

I nodded. "Very much so."

"Then why didn't you ask me again?"

"Because you said no." I tossed a hand into the air, the hold on my temper nearly a thread. "I got the message. Over and over. You're leaving Summers and not looking back. I'm not the type of guy who asks a question when I already know the answer."

"Oh." She lifted a hand to cover a smile.

I reached across the truck and pulled that hand away. "You're not leaving?"

"I'm not leaving. I was looking for a place to turn around when that truck tried to run me off the road."

But she'd been so set on going. "For how long?"

"I haven't really put a time limit on this. Would you mind if I stayed?" She paused. "With you?"

Would I mind? Fuck no, I wouldn't mind. She could stay with me for as long as she wanted. Forever, if that suited her fancy. With Londyn, each day was brighter. I didn't want to live the rest of my life alone. But I didn't want just any woman to share my life.

I wanted Londyn.

Something I wanted to talk about, but not while I was driving a goddamn tow truck.

"Hold that question for me, honey. I need to see your face."

She nodded, folding her hands in her lap. Damn it. Had that come out as a rejection? Because that's not what I'd meant.

Son of a bitch. I was pissed about the asshole who'd run her off the road and things weren't coming out right. I hit the edge of Summers and pulled the rig to the side of the road. Then I hopped out, jogging around to the other side to open Londyn's door. "Climb down."

She nodded, undoing her seat belt. Then she stepped on the running board before jumping to the road.

"Start over for me. You're staying?" I needed to hear it again.

Londyn nodded. "I'd like to stay."

"And I'd like you to stay. With me."

"Yes, please." She giggled.

I wrapped her up, pulling her into my chest. Then I laughed with her, long and loud.

She was staying.

"What made you change your mind?" I asked, dropping my cheek to the top of her head.

"The truth? I'm scared."

I let her go, taking her chin under my finger to tip up her face. "Why?"

"I've always been the one to leave."

One sentence, and it all made sense. Running away was how Londyn stayed in control. It was her protection mechanism. "I get it."

"What if you leave me?" Sheer vulnerability washed

over her face. She stripped away all the guards, making her even more beautiful. "I've never stuck around to see the pieces fall apart. I don't know if I'm strong enough to take it."

"I'm not going anywhere, honey. If you stay, we're going to make a real thing out of this. Mark my words."

"How do you know?"

I took her hand and placed it over my heart, then I covered it with my own. "I feel it. Deep."

Londyn wasn't in the place to hear three little words, not yet. Hell, I wasn't ready to say them. But there wasn't a rush. We had time.

Because she was staying.

I took her mouth in a kiss, sweeping my tongue against hers for the taste I'd crave for the rest of my life. This was a big risk on her part, and I'd make sure she never regretted it. She'd never second-guess a life in Summers.

I broke the kiss and dropped my forehead to hers. "This is a better end to the day than I'd expected."

"Me too. Except for the whacko who ran me off the road."

I muttered a curse. "Let's get home."

She nodded and let me help her up into the truck.

"Want to come along with me to the shop?" I asked, easing onto the road. "Or sit at the motel with Meggie? I don't care either way, I just don't want you alone."

"I'd like to stay with you." She shivered, reaching over

for my hand. The fear she'd been hiding was leeching through her calm exterior.

"This has gone too far. The vandalism was one thing, but you could have been hurt."

"Who would do this to me?" she whispered. "I don't know anyone in Summers."

"I don't think this is about you. It's got to be about me."

"Well, it's not Moira. So what other enemies do you have in town?"

"Hell if I know." Up until today, I would have said I was a fairly well-liked guy. I got along with most folks in town. My entire family was well liked too. I couldn't think of the last time I'd had an unhappy customer at the shop.

It didn't take us long to get to the shop, but unloading the car took some time. When it was in its regular stall, we both walked around the Cadillac, taking in all the damage. It wasn't horrible, but it wasn't a quick fix either.

"Mack's going to be able to send his kids to college on all the money he's making to fix this Cadillac."

Londyn laughed, leaning against me. "It's only seven o'clock but I'm so ready for bed."

"Dinner first. What would you like?"

"Pizza."

"Pizza it is." I nodded. "I'll call Wyatt and have him bring one over for us."

"He's not at Moira's tonight?"

"He is, but if I tell him you're staying indefinitely, he'll come with an extra-large meat supreme."

She smiled up at me. "With the veggies."

"With the veggies."

"It looks so sad." Her eyes raked over the car, the scratches and the dents. It would take considerably longer at the body shop to repair this wreck. It might even require some new parts.

"I'll fix it," I vowed. "Then . . ." I'd gotten so used to saying that she'd be on her way.

"Then I'll drive it around Summers."

"What about returning it to Karson? What about taking it to California?"

She lifted a shoulder. "Someday, I'd like to track him down. I'd like to give him this car and let him have it for a while. But maybe when that time comes, you'll come with me."

"I'd like that."

"We could wait until Wyatt is in college. If we pick a time when you can be away from the garage, maybe that wish I made might actually come true."

"You're sure?" I put my hands on her shoulders. "You'll wait? You'll stay in Summers until then?"

"I'm staying. Would you come with me to California?"

"Yes." Without a doubt. Londyn would have a hard time taking a trip across the country without me. "That's a lot of long-term thinking for a woman who just wanted to roam America."

Londyn laughed. "I want to roam, just not alone."

"Turns out I haven't had a decent vacation in sixteen years. Think I'm overdue."

"California first. Then where?"

I let out a long breath. "Are we really talking about this? You and me?"

"I feel it." She put her hand over her own heart this time. "Deep."

"Then California first. We'll decide where to go from there."

She crashed into my arms, winding her arms around my waist. I breathed in her scent, grateful I wouldn't have to search for it on the sheets tonight because she was here. I could hold her. Touch her.

Keep her.

We stood there, holding on to one another, until her stomach rumbled and forced us apart. "Let's get home. We'll eat and then call it a day."

The police would likely have a ton of questions tomorrow. All I cared about was that they found the person who did this.

Londyn unwrapped herself from around me and stepped away, taking another crushing look at her car.

I turned too, inspecting it once more. It was a fucking mess. The paint was scratched to hell. A couple of the panels were dented. The mirror on the passenger side was barely hanging on. The bumper was loose.

"What color was the truck again?" I asked. She'd told

the deputy, but I'd been so fucking furious and scared, I hadn't absorbed the details.

"Blue."

"What kind of blue?"

She shrugged. "I don't know. Bright. Electric blue, maybe?"

Electric blue. "And what kind of truck? Do you remember any details?"

"No, not really. I just remember it was really tall. When it was beside me, I couldn't see inside."

An electric blue truck with a lift kit.

I'd seen a truck like that parked in my own driveway more than once.

"What the hell?" I stood, fisting my hands on my hips. No way.

"What?" Londyn came to my side, staring at the spot where I was looking. "What am I looking at?"

"You're sure it was bright blue?"

"Yes." She nodded.

I snatched up her hand and marched for the back door. I hit the button to close the overhead door and locked up as soon as we were outside. Then I put us both in my truck, not uttering a word.

My mind was stuck on a possibility I didn't even want to consider.

"Okay, what am I missing?" Londyn asked as I backed away from the garage.

"A hunch," I answered through gritted teeth. And if that hunch was right, I was about to lose my shit.

I sped down the streets toward home, skidding to a stop when I hit my driveway. The second Londyn and I were out of the car, I whipped out my phone and dialed my son's number.

"Hey, Dad," he answered.

"Get home. Now." I ended the call without explanation.

"What's going on, Brooks?" Londyn touched my forearm as I paced on the grass beyond the front door.

"Describe it all to me again. Start at the beginning."

"Okay." She took a deep breath. "The truck came up behind me while I was on the phone with Gemma. I didn't even see it until it was right behind me, and only then all I could really see was the grill. I was trying to watch the road. It bumped me a couple of times, then drove up beside me. I thought it would pass, but it stayed close. There was a car coming the other way so I hit the brakes. I swerved, overcorrected and veered into the ditch."

"When the truck was beside you, what did it look like?"

She shrugged. "I don't know. Tall, mostly. Blue. It wasn't shiny though, not like the Cadillac."

Matte electric blue. I was seconds away from nuclear, but I kept it together because I didn't want to scare Londyn. "Okay. What else? Did you see the driver?"

"No. I was just trying to stay on the road."

"Understandable. Was there someone else? A passenger? Or was it only the driver?"

Her forehead furrowed as she thought it over. "I-I don't know."

We'd find out soon enough.

I stayed in the front yard, my arms crossed over my chest, until Wyatt drove up in his white Ford F-150. We'd bought the truck about six months ago on his birthday. He'd chipped in a third from his savings, and I'd covered the rest.

If I was right, that truck was about to become a lawn ornament.

"Hey." He stepped out and waved to Londyn. "You're back."

She opened her mouth to answer, but before she could speak, I held up a hand. "Truth, son. I expect the truth."

That's all I had to say. His frame crumpled. "It wasn't my idea."

"Fuck." I ran a hand through my hair. "What the fuck were you thinking?"

"It was Joe's idea."

Fucking Joe. An idiot of a kid who, at best, had two brain cells to rub together. The kid came from absentee parents who thought restoring an old Chevy truck, complete with a monster lift kit and custom paint job, was the way to their son's heart.

"Joe's idea. That's not a reason!" I roared. "You could have hurt her. You could have killed her."

Wyatt's face paled. "We were just trying to scare her. Joe wasn't supposed to run her off the road, just tap her bumper a couple of times. Scare her into turning around."

"Oh, Wyatt." Londyn touched her hand to her heart. "It was you?"

My son's frame sank even lower as he hung his head. "I'm sorry."

"Why?" I demanded, my fury barely in check. How could my son do this to me? How could he put the woman I loved—absolutely fucking loved after only weeks—in danger like that?

"You seemed happy," Wyatt whispered. "I saw you on the rock together. That night I delivered Thai to Meggie. I forgot her extra carton of rice, so I brought it over. You were laughing. I thought, if she stayed longer, you might . . . I don't know."

He thought I'd stay happy.

So he'd vandalized the garage. He'd slashed her tires. He'd done it all to get Londyn to stay.

My anger dulled from a raging boil to a hot simmer. "Son, this was not the way."

"I know." He hung his head. "I just . . . I was trying to help."

Christ. I cast a glance at Londyn. She wasn't even mad. She stared at Wyatt with a soft smile on her face. "You might have hurt her. Things could have ended much differently."

"I told him not to hit her car. I told him over and over

to back off. But he didn't listen." He lifted his head to Londyn. "I'm so sorry. I saw you swerve into the ditch and I've never been more scared. I begged Joe to go back for you, but he said the cops would arrest us. Are you okay?"

"I'm okay." Londyn sighed. "Scared, but otherwise unharmed."

Goddamn it. I rubbed my temples. What was I supposed to do now? I pulled out my phone from my pocket and handed it to Wyatt.

"Call the sheriff's station. You can explain what happened."

Wyatt's face twisted in agony, but he nodded. "Okay, Dad."

Then I stood there and watched my son make probably the hardest phone call of his life.

The deputy who'd been on the road with us came over and took our statements along with Wyatt's confession. Londyn refused to press charges. An hour later, Wyatt had been issued a warning and the deputy was on his way to Joe's house to deliver a reckless driving ticket.

It was a slap on the wrist, but one I knew would sink deep for my son.

"I'm sorry, Dad," Wyatt said as we sat in the living room. We still hadn't eaten, but I'd lost my appetite. I'd offered to get a pizza delivered, but Londyn hadn't been hungry anymore either.

"You're grounded. Until . . . college." Maybe longer.

"I'm assuming the keying and the tires and wrecking the garage was you too?"

He gave me a solemn nod.

Wyatt was the other person with a key to the garage and the thought that he'd do that to me or a customer hadn't even crossed my mind. "You're paying me back for everything. With interest."

He hung his head. "Yes, sir."

Londyn's hand came over mine as she shifted closer on the couch. She looked up at me, her eyes begging me to take it easy.

Maybe I would, but I certainly wouldn't tonight. Vehicles were weapons. I'd taught that lesson to Wyatt many times, so why hadn't he learned? And the vandalism? That was petty bullshit. I'd raised him better than that.

And as far as I was concerned, Wyatt wasn't hanging out with Joe for the rest of his life.

"Go to bed," I ordered. I'd already texted Moira what was going on. Thankfully, she'd always been in sync with me as a parent. We supported one another when it came to punishments for Wyatt.

She'd promised that while he was grounded at my house, he'd be grounded at hers too.

Wyatt stood from the chair, turning for his room, but before he walked away, he came over to Londyn, bending low to give her a hug. "Sorry."

She patted his shoulder. "Good night, Wyatt."

He sulked to his bedroom.

When his door was closed, I let my head fall back into the couch. "Shit. He did it for the right reasons, but damn. I don't even know what to say."

Londyn stayed quiet for a minute, then her hand flew to her mouth. I sat up, expecting tears. Instead, she had a fit of giggles. Her hand muffled the laughter, but her eyes watered.

"Is this really funny?"

She pulled herself together, swiping her eyes dry. "Do you think we should tell him I was turning around anyway?"

"Yes," I muttered. "He needs to suffer for his stupidity."

"But not too much." She curled into my side. "His heart was in the right place."

"Yeah." He'd been thinking of his dad. He'd seen right from the start, before even knowing her, that Londyn was someone special. "I didn't get your suitcases from the Cadillac."

"I don't think I need any clothes tonight, do you?"

Tonight. Tomorrow night. All the nights after that. "No, you don't."

We'd get her suitcases tomorrow, she'd unload them into my closet, and she'd stay. She might not realize it yet, but she was home. In Summers. In this house.

The next time she wanted to leave and find a new adventure, she'd have company.

We'd drive that runaway road together.

EPILOGUE

O *ne year later . . .*
    "I'm going to the store. Need anything?"

"No," Brooks said from beneath a gray Chevy Silverado, where he was changing the oil. "Wait. Yeah, I need shaving cream."

"Anything else?" I gave him a minute to think it over. I knew there was more. There was always more. The man never seemed to remember what he needed when I was making my list, but five minutes before I left for the store, he'd rattle off four or five items.

"Flossers."

"And?" I swung the car seat at my side, glancing down at our daughter. Ellie Cohen was fast asleep, a binky dangling from her pink lips.

"Orange juice."

I already had that one on my list. "And?"

235

"Uh . . ."

I sighed and looked at Tony. He stood against a tool box, his chest shaking in silent laughter. Brooks and I didn't just have this standoff for the grocery store. He'd always tack on a handful of parts right before I was ready to hit send on the order.

"I'm leaving in four, three, two—"

"Pickles."

My face soured. Thanks to my unexpected pregnancy and a horrible bout of morning sickness, pickles were no longer on my favorite foods list. But I'd buy them for Brooks because he loved them on his ham sandwiches. "Okay, we're taking off. I'll meet you at home."

"Drive careful."

"I will," I promised like I did each time he sent me off with the same warning. "Don't be late. You have one hour to get home and get showered before we need to leave."

Wyatt had his first football game of the season tonight and he was starting as linebacker. He was nervous—something I found exceptionally endearing—because the girl he'd been crushing on was going to be in the stands watching.

Wyatt was still grounded, both at Brooks's house and at Moira's, but it was coming to an end. One year of near angelic behavior and his parents were struggling to punish him any longer. If it had been my decision, he would have been forgiven months ago.

"Don't worry, honey. I'll be there."

Okay, maybe I was just as nervous for tonight's game as Wyatt. "Love you," I called.

Brooks, lying on his back on a wheeled cart, pushed out from under the Chevy and grinned. "Love you too."

I blew him a kiss, waved goodbye to Tony, then headed out the back door, where my Cadillac waited. She gleamed in the September sunshine, her color coordinating with autumn's turning leaves. But I wasn't driving her around Summers today. Brooks would bring home the Cadillac and I was taking his truck—it was safer for Ellie and her car seat.

It had taken a month to get the Cadillac fixed after the crash into the ditch. It hadn't mattered much to me, considering anywhere I needed to go, Brooks was more than willing to drive me.

My first month as an official resident of Summers was spent waking up with the sunshine each morning and falling asleep beside Brooks each night. More often than not, I found myself at the garage during the day, where I stayed in the office while Brooks and Tony worked on cars.

The stack of paperwork in Brooks's office called my name. I asked for the password to his computer and figured out the rest myself, only asking questions when necessary.

Though I was already doing the work, when Brooks offered me the job as office manager, I hesitated to accept. Was I repeating the same pattern from Boston? It took me a week to work past those fears and realize they were unfounded.

Life in Summers was nothing like Boston. Brooks was nothing like Thomas.

He hadn't offered me a job with *his* company. He hadn't given me a home in *his* house.

Everything about our life was *ours*.

Brooks added my name to the title on the house. I bought into the garage as his partner.

Summers was home, but Brooks and I talked often about where we'd go exploring. We had a few years between Wyatt's graduation from high school and the time Ellie would start kindergarten.

Our plan was to take as many vacations as we could afford until it was time to put her in school. Then we'd limit travel to summers. Maybe Wyatt would come too, depending on his college schedule, and we'd make it a family trip.

Ellie was a beautiful surprise.

She was one month old and the anchor of my heart.

Brooks and I hadn't planned on getting pregnant. We hadn't even talked about marriage until that fateful day when I'd held a positive pregnancy test in my hand as joyous tears streamed down my face. But somewhere along the way, a condom hadn't worked, and like all things with our relationship, we'd moved into the future at warp speed.

The two of us had married in his parents' yard beside

the lake two weeks later. Then we'd waited for Ellie to arrive. The day she was born was the day I'd learned true peace.

I'd learned unconditional love.

I vowed never to fail her the way my parents had failed me.

After a lot of thought, I'd decided to investigate my parents in the hopes it would mend those dark, open wounds. They'd died days after I'd run away—a dual heroin overdose. My parents had been found together in their bed. Maybe if they had survived, they would have come looking for me.

Maybe not.

For now, I took comfort in knowing their tortured souls were at rest. And that running away had put me on a path that ultimately led home.

I felt it. Deep.

The trip to the grocery store was uneventful. Ellie stayed asleep even as the cashier fawned over her precious face. And she slept until we were home, unloading groceries into the kitchen.

"Hi, baby," I cooed as she woke with a yawn. I hauled her out of the car seat just as the doorbell rang. "Should we go see who's here?"

Ellie tooted.

I laughed, walking to the door. I opened it up, expecting Meggie or a neighbor, but my jaw dropped at the woman on my porch. "Gemma?"

"Hi." She tugged off her sunglasses. "Surprise."

"Yes, it sure is." I smiled, waving her inside. "What are you doing here?"

Her eyes flooded. "I ran away."

———

"SHE'S BEAUTIFUL. TRULY." Gemma touched her finger to the top of Ellie's nose.

"I think so." I smiled, watching my friend cuddle my daughter as we sat on the back deck.

Last night after Gemma had arrived, she'd given me the quick and dirty details of leaving Boston, but we hadn't had time to talk. Brooks had shown up twenty minutes after Gemma and we'd all rushed to the football game.

When we'd gotten home, I'd nursed Ellie, then Brooks had put her to bed while Gemma and I had spent a solid three hours on the couch, talking. We'd picked right back up again this morning.

"You're right. This is amazing iced coffee."

I took a sip of my own. "Told you so."

"If Meggie had a spa, I might just stay in Summers forever." Gemma had opted for the motel instead of our guest bedroom, wanting to give us privacy. Meggie had put her in my old room, number five.

It was good to see her in a pair of faded jeans and a loose green sweater. Her feet were in flimsy sandals. I hadn't seen her relaxed like this in years.

Since I'd moved to Summers, Gemma and I had spoken on the phone every few weeks. She'd traveled to West Virginia for my wedding but hadn't been back since Ellie was born.

"You found it," Gemma said, staring out at the lake.

"Found what?"

"A real life."

I followed her gaze to the water. "Yes, I did."

Brooks and Wyatt were on the dock, tinkering with something on the boat. Brooks must have felt my stare because he looked up and waved. The smile tugging at his lips was likely the same one that had gotten me pregnant.

"I want a real life, Lonny."

I put my hand on her forearm. "You're sure leaving Boston is the right call?"

"I'm sure." She tipped her head to the sky. "But I still can't believe I did it. That I left it all behind."

Last night, she'd told me that she'd sold her company, her house and her car. She'd kept her investments in other ventures that required little to no work, but as of yesterday, she was unemployed and homeless.

Wealthy, but homeless nonetheless.

"I don't know where I belong," she confessed. "I think when you were in Boston and I was working so much, it was easy to pretend I was where I needed to be. But I'm alone. I've been alone since we were kids."

I'd had a miserable childhood, but Gemma's made mine seem like a fairy tale.

241

"I figured I'd give West Virginia a try for a few days until I decide where to go next," she said, turning her attention again to Ellie. "Worked for you."

"True." I kept my gaze on my husband.

Brooks and Wyatt had the fishing poles out now. The two of them had been spending more and more time together as of late. Wyatt still went to spend every other week with Moira, but every weekend, he was here with Brooks. They were putting in time together while they still had it. Wyatt was being scouted by four different college teams, and before we blinked, he'd be gone.

Brooks looked to the house again, once more catching my eye. This time, I waved. His handsome face was rough with stubble, his hair windblown and unruly. My heart skipped.

"Ugh," Gemma groaned. "You're almost impossible to be around right now. You two are worse than you and Karson as kids."

"I'm not even sorry." I giggled. "He's the best thing that ever happened to me."

"I'm happy for you."

I smiled. "Me too. What will you do?"

"I don't have the faintest damn idea."

Maybe I did. I held up a hand. "Wait here."

I hurried through the house for the kitchen, finding Brooks's keys. I twisted off the two I needed and when I returned to the porch, I found Brooks at the table next to Gemma. He'd stolen Ellie from her.

"Here." I tossed Gemma the keys to the Cadillac.

She caught them. "What are these?"

"The keys to the Cadillac. Take it. When you find him, tell Karson thanks."

Gemma studied the keys, then closed them in her grip. "Thanks for what?"

I took in Brooks, who was smiling at our daughter.

"For leading me home."

———

The Runaway series continues with Wild Highway.

WILD HIGHWAY

Gemma Lane built an empire. Not a small feat, considering her home as a teenager was a makeshift tent in a California junkyard. She's dedicated her life to turning pennies into millions. She has power, fortune and prestige.

And she's leaving it all behind.

Gemma is headed across the country in her best friend's Cadillac when a detour in Montana reunites her with old acquaintances and a man who hasn't changed. Easton Greer challenges her every word and tests her every limit because he doesn't believe she's really abandoned her riches. She ignores his snide remarks and muttered censure—until the day she's ready to return to the wild highway, and Easton taunts her to stay.

She'll prove to him she's not just running back to her wealthy life, that she's more than her money. She'll unlock her guarded heart and hope that this time around, he'll treasure the key.

ACKNOWLEDGMENTS

Thank you for reading *Runaway Road*! This series is a passion project of mine, inspired by a daydream I had one day when organizing my bookshelf.

When I was a kid, I loved reading. My favorite "chapter books" were The Boxcar Children. Over the years, I've been collecting them, hoping one day my own kids would love them as much as I did. One day I was in my office, staring at my bookshelf and lost in thought, when I spotted the spines for that series and wondered what happened to those kids as adults. From there, Londyn and her junkyard friends were born. I can't wait to introduce you to the others as the series continues.

Special thanks to my editing and proofreading team: Elizabeth Nover, Lauren Clarke, Julie Deaton, Karen Lawson and Judy Zweifel. Thank you to Sarah Hansen for the beautiful cover. And thank you to my publicist, Danielle Sanchez.

Thank you to all the members of Perry Street for being the best superfans I could ask for. Thank you to the incredible bloggers who read and spread the word about my books. And thank you to my friends and my wonderful family for your unconditional love and support.

ABOUT THE AUTHOR

Devney is a *USA Today* bestselling author who lives in Washington with her husband and two sons. Born and raised in Montana, she loves writing books set in her treasured home state. After working in the technology industry for nearly a decade, she abandoned conference calls and project schedules to enjoy a slower pace at home with her family. Writing one book, let alone many, was not something she ever expected to do. But now that she's discovered her true passion for writing romance, she has no plans to ever stop.

Don't miss out on Devney's latest book news.
Subscribe to her newsletter!
www.devneyperry.com

Printed in Great Britain
by Amazon